Caress of Pleasure

Also From JK

Erotic romance

As Julie Kenner
Caress of Darkness
Find Me in Darkness
Find Me in Pleasure
Find Me in Passion
Caress of Pleasure

As J. Kenner
Stark Series novels
Release Me (a New York Times and USA Today bestseller)
Claim Me (a #2 New York Times bestseller!)
Complete Me (a #2 New York Times bestseller!)

Stark Ever After novellas
Take Me
Have Me
Play My Game

Stark International novels
Say My Name
On My Knees
Under My Skin

Stark International novellas
Tame Me

The Most Wanted series
Wanted
Heated
Ignited

Other Genres

Kate Connor Demon-Hunting Soccer Mom Series (suburban fantasy/paranormal)
Carpe Demon
California Demon
Demons Are Forever
The Demon You Know

Caress of Pleasure

A Dark Pleasures Novella

By Julie Kenner

1001 Dark Nights

EVIL EYE

CONCEPTS

Caress of Pleasure
A Dark Pleasures Novella
By Julie Kenner

Copyright 2015 Julie Kenner
ISBN: 978-1-940887-53-1

Foreword: Copyright 2014 M. J. Rose

Published by Evil Eye Concepts, Incorporated

Sign up for the 1001 Dark Nights Newsletter
and be entered to win a Tiffany Key necklace.

There's a contest every month!

Go to www.1001DarkNights.com to subscribe.

As a bonus, all subscribers will receive a free
1001 Dark Nights story
The First Night
by Lexi Blake & M.J. Rose

One Thousand and One Dark Nights

Once upon a time, in the future…

*I was a student fascinated with stories and learning.
I studied philosophy, poetry, history, the occult, and
the art and science of love and magic. I had a vast
library at my father's home and collected thousands
of volumes of fantastic tales.*

*I learned all about ancient races and bygone
times. About myths and legends and dreams of all
people through the millennium. And the more I read
the stronger my imagination grew until I discovered
that I was able to travel into the stories… to actually
become part of them.*

*I wish I could say that I listened to my teacher
and respected my gift, as I ought to have. If I had, I
would not be telling you this tale now.
But I was foolhardy and confused, showing off
with bravery.*

*One afternoon, curious about the myth of the
Arabian Nights, I traveled back to ancient Persia to
see for myself if it was true that every day Shahryar
(Persian: شهریار, "king") married a new virgin, and then
sent yesterday's wife to be beheaded. It was written
and I had read, that by the time he met Scheherazade,
the vizier's daughter, he'd killed one thousand
women.*

*Something went wrong with my efforts. I arrived
in the midst of the story and somehow exchanged
places with Scheherazade — a phenomena that had
never occurred before and that still to this day, I
cannot explain.*

*Now I am trapped in that ancient past. I have
taken on Scheherazade's life and the only way I can
protect myself and stay alive is to do what she did to
protect herself and stay alive.*

*Every night the King calls for me and listens as I spin tales.
And when the evening ends and dawn breaks, I stop at a
point that leaves him breathless and yearning for more.
And so the King spares my life for one more day, so that
he might hear the rest of my dark tale.*

*As soon as I finish a story... I begin a new
one... like the one that you, dear reader, have before
you now.*

Chapter 1

Dante strode through the members' area of Dark Pleasures, ignoring the coy looks from two women, both of whom he'd fucked within the last six months. He wasn't interested in them. Hell, he wasn't even interested in the exceptionally nubile young actress who'd spent the last two nights in his bed. Or in the curvy detective who'd warmed his sheets for three days before that.

His fling with that leggy gallery owner had lasted almost two weeks, but he'd known it was doomed from the beginning. There was never a real spark, and when he'd caught his mind wandering while she was sucking his cock, he knew that it was time to move on.

He was drowning in a sea of women, and he'd never been more lonely.

Damn, but he was fucked up.

With a sigh, he paused in front of the long mahogany bar. He turned, leaning back against it and letting the soft strains of music from the five-piece orchestra in the corner drift over him. After a moment, Gregory, the club's newly hired bartender, approached from behind. "Anything for you, sir?"

Dante shook his head. "I'm not staying. Not tonight." He turned to face the younger man. Twenty-six, an aspiring actor. He was a recent hire and had the bearing and respectful attitude that did the members-only club credit.

As one of the owners, Dante spent a great deal of time in this room, chatting up members at the bar, discussing literature in the corners while smoking a fine cigar and sipping scotch. Flirting with the women in the shadows, and then inviting a select few back to his brownstone next door.

It had become a routine, sometimes a pleasure. Always a distraction.

Tonight, he wanted none of it.

Although, actually, he did want a drink. Five or six, even. Just not here.

One of the women—Lisa? Liesl?—tried to catch his attention as he pushed away from the bar, but he passed her without comment as he moved with purpose to the far side of the room, then punched his code into the keypad to enter the private VIP area, exclusive only to Dark Pleasures' owners and their special guests.

He stepped inside, relieved to be away from the crowd, to not have to be on his best behavior. And to not have to watch every tiny word he said, lest he give some inadvertent hint that Dark Pleasures—and the men who owned it—weren't exactly as they seemed.

The decor in the VIP lounge was similar to that in the main area—stunning paintings, comfortable furniture, leather and wood, and the kind of dim lighting that gave the place a smoky feel appropriate for an establishment that focused on fine liquor and even finer cigars.

But unlike the members' area, the lounge had an additional quality of casual camaraderie. Of coming home. Because to the men and women of the Phoenix Brotherhood, this place really was a second home. Certainly, it was where they gathered to be with family.

Here, no bartender was needed, and Dante headed straight to the bar, grabbed one of the whiskey glasses, and poured himself two fingers of Glenmorangie.

He kept his back to the room, letting the voices of his friends in the brotherhood drift over him. Liam, Mal, Raine. And the women, Jessica and Callie and Christina. He hadn't seen Dagny when he entered, and he didn't hear her now.

He wasn't surprised. She'd been spending time with a mortal—Christina's old roommate and best friend. And while Dagny swore it wasn't serious, Dante could see that hungry look in her eyes—and oh, dear Christ, he pitied her. He'd fallen for a mortal, after all. And after thirteen years, the memory of Brenna Hart still had the power to wreck him.

Hell, it was wrecking him right now.

Fuck.

He pushed through the melancholy, forcing it out of his mind by checking out and just letting the sounds and scents flow through him some more. The drift of conversation. The clink of ice in glasses. That uniquely sweet scent of scotch mixed with the pungent tang of fine cigars. Even in his current mood, it was soothing.

Hell, it was home.

Of course, not everyone was around. Asher and Trace were both out of the country this week, and Pieter, who had spent the last twenty years heading up the Bangkok office, was busy moving into the guest apartment until he decided where he wanted to settle in Manhattan.

Slowly, Dante rolled his neck, working out the kinks. Then he tossed back the scotch and poured himself another.

A moment later, Raine edged up beside him, grabbed the bottle, and poured a glass of his own. Dante glanced at his friend from the corner of his eye.

Raine ran a hand over his close-shaved head, sighed, and then took a long swallow before shifting his stance to prop his elbow on the bar and focus that razor-sharp attention on Dante.

For centuries, Raine had walked with a shadow. Hell, he'd

seemed dead, which was damned ironic considering he was immortal. But that shadow had dissipated months ago. Now, Raine practically burst with life. And Dante knew the reason—Callie. Raine had been reunited with his mate, and while Dante was happy as shit for his friend, he was also so goddamn fucking jealous he was making himself crazy.

Shit.

He poured again. He drank again.

And then he refilled his glass one more time.

Beside him, Raine eyed him impassively. "Bad day?"

"Bad century," Dante said, then corrected himself. "No, bad thirteen years. Fuck." He tossed back the last of his drink, then grabbed the bottle.

"Dante..."

Raine's voice held an edge of understanding, and Dante cringed. Truth was, if anyone understood it would be Raine. For thousands of years Raine had been alone, believing his love was lost forever. So, yeah, maybe he got it.

But right now, Dante didn't care about understanding. He didn't care about pity. He wanted only one thing, and that was something he couldn't have.

He'd tossed Brenna away with both hands thirteen years ago because it was impossible, and though he knew he'd done the right thing, every few years the weight of the loss seemed to add up until it finally pushed him down and he had to just give in and wallow.

Tomorrow, he'd find another woman to take the edge off. Tonight, he'd lie in bed, drink, and remember.

"Come on, man," Raine said. "Mal's got a call with London so he's not up for a game of chess, but I could use one.

"I'm not good company tonight."

"Planning a bender?"

"Gonna do my best." Considering his—and all the brotherhood's—remarkable ability to heal, getting drunk really wasn't in the cards. But if he tossed back shot after shot, maybe he could at least get a little buzz on. Right now, the prospect was pretty damned appealing.

"You wanna talk about it?"

Dante actually chuckled. Raine was a damn good friend, but touchy-feely he wasn't. If he was offering Dante the chance to spill his emotional debris all over the polished wooden floor, then Dante must look more wrecked than he'd thought.

He glanced across the room and saw Callie, Raine's mate. His wife. The woman he'd been bound to thousands of years ago— and at the same time the woman he'd known for only a few months. And there was Mal, sitting on the leather sofa talking into his phone while Christina curled up beside him, her feet on his lap as she read a book. They'd been reunited after thousands of years apart. Mated. Bound.

Fated.

And as for Liam and Jessica, they'd been side-by-side for three thousand years, and now she was whispering something in his ear and he had his arm around her waist, and it was all just so goddamn fucking perfect that Dante—

"No," he said firmly. "I don't want to talk about it."

No way was he shitting all over his friends' happiness.

Better to try and drown his troubles. Or at least take a long nap. He lifted the bottle as if in salute. "I'll be back to myself tomorrow. Tonight, I'm just a little fucked up. You'll excuse me. I need to go valiantly try to drink myself into oblivion. I'll fail, but I'm up for the challenge."

* * * *

"Dante, hold up a second!"

Mal's voice rang out from across the room, and Dante swallowed a curse before he turned around to face his friend, who also happened to be the co-leader of the brotherhood along with

Liam. But leader or not, Dante was going to tell Mal that whatever it was could wait until morning.

Or he was going to say that until he saw the look on Mal's face. Shock and grief and the gray sheen of past pain. And underneath that, Dante saw just the slightest hint of hope.

Just like that, he tossed away his plan to spend a long evening with a bottle and his memories. And he headed across the room toward his friend.

Malcolm Greer was a man good at hiding his emotions—god knows he'd had enough years of practice.

Tonight, he wasn't even trying. Christina had sat up and was leaning against him, and Mal was holding her close as if she was a lifeline, his gray eyes full of storm clouds.

"Talk to me," Dante said even as Raine and Liam joined them.

"What's going—"

But Raine's question was cut off by Liam's gruff, "So it's true."

Mal nodded, just one quick affirmative motion.

"Dammit, Mal," Dante said. "What's true?"

"Merrick," Mal said. "He's alive."

It was the last thing that Dante had expected to hear, and he reached blindly for the armrest of the chair behind him. He sank into it, barely even noticing the motion, as he glanced over at Raine, who appeared about as shell-shocked as Dante felt.

"Merrick?" Dante repeated, just in case he was having a sudden attack of insanity. "You're talking about our Merrick?"

Merrick had been one of their team when the brotherhood had crash-landed in this dimension and on this planet so many millennia ago. He'd been one of their strongest warriors, but the battle with the fuerie—the enemy they'd been chasing across dimensions—had been brutal, and he'd been thrust back into the void, his essence dispersed. *Dead.* Or at least as dead as a creature made of pure energy could be.

"Apparently he didn't go into the void." Mal's voice was flat. Harsh. "He was captured. And all this time we didn't have a fucking clue."

"Captured?" Raine repeated. "But—how? Where? It's been three thousand years, how could they—?"

"A gemstone," Liam said softly, and Dante nodded in understanding. Gemstones held and channeled energy—that was one reason they were often used by mortals to heal—and because of that energy, they could also be used to bind creatures like the fuerie and those in the brotherhood.

"A few weeks ago, Christina noticed something odd during her morning scan," Mal said, picking up the thread of conversation. "A blip—something off in the energy pattern that she was seeing in the London area." He glanced at Christina for confirmation.

"I wasn't sure what I was seeing," she said. "And then it was gone. And I didn't see it again for a few more days."

Everyone in the brotherhood had unique skills, but Christina's were especially honed, the remnant of having suffered her own torment at the hand of the fuerie. Now, she had the ability to see a map of the world in her mind. And that map showed her not only the fuerie's energy, but the energy from certain gemstones, and also the energy of the brothers' themselves. She'd discovered the latter after a few months of practicing her skill, and it had proved handy for keeping tabs on members of the brotherhood who were out on missions.

"You saw Merrick's energy," Raine said.

"Yes and no. It was strange. Like the energy of a gemstone, but with a hint of the brotherhood, too. I didn't understand it, and at first neither did Mal."

"It took us a while to figure out what she was seeing, but we have confirmation now—Merrick didn't go into the void. He's trapped in a gemstone and has been for millennia. And now it's our job to get him out."

"Holy fuck," Dante said. "You're certain?"

Liam nodded. "We are. Merrick and Livia were the only two who went unwitnessed into the void. We assumed. We were wrong." He looked at Raine as he spoke. Livia had been his mate and for millennia, he'd believed he had lost her, only to learn that she had escaped the void by merging her essence with a human's. And that human turned out to be one of Callie's ancestors.

"I won't go into everything we've done since Christina first saw the hint of his essence," Mal put in. "The bottom line is that he was trapped inside a gemstone—presumably by the fuerie. That stone ended up in a gem-encrusted brooch owned by various royal families."

"The brooch is in the shape of a phoenix." Liam's mouth curved into an ironic smile. The brotherhood had come to call themselves the Phoenix Brotherhood specifically because of the unique manifestation of their mortality. They could be killed, yes, but they were born again in fire.

"Coincidence?" Raine asked.

Christina shook her head. "I don't think so. As far as we know, the fuerie don't know how to shield a gemstone's energy. But this stone seems to be shielded. When we were tracing the provenance, we saw that the brooch came into existence in the fourteenth century. Before that, the stone was in an ancient Egyptian ornament. But during the Renaissance, an artisan worked it into the brooch. And that artisan had a reputation as a sorcerer."

"Of the fuerie?" Dante asked

"More likely one of the rare humans who understands energy the way we do," Mal said. "Perhaps he discovered a way. Perhaps the fuerie hired him to make the brooch—and to shield it."

"We may never know for certain," Christina said. "But the bottom line is that it disappears from the map periodically, but then pops up again. The shield is wearing off. And that means we can find it. We can acquire it."

"Where is it?" Dante asked.

"It went recently into the private market and Michael Folsom hired an intermediary to acquire it on his behalf," Liam said, referring to a local Manhattan billionaire who had a penchant for collecting unusual things.

"Are the fuerie after it?"

"I don't know," Christina said. "They may have lost interest centuries ago. It's floated around museums and private collections. It's in the city now, but I haven't detected the fuerie in this area in weeks." She looked at Dante. "Have you?"

He shook his head. His power was nowhere near as strong as Christina's, but he was constantly reaching out, searching his surroundings for the slightest hint that the fuerie were nearby.

"And we're certain that it's Merrick in this gemstone?"

Liam and Mal exchanged glances. "As confident as we can be until we free him," Mal said. "But we're also confident that time is short. His essence is escaping—and we've confirmed that the stone has acquired a flaw, and I think his essence is being pulled out. He's fighting to remain, but if he's drawn fully out into the ether..."

"Then his essence will be dissipated throughout the universe, and we'll lose the consciousness that we know as Merrick forever." Dante sighed. "Well, fuck."

"How much time?" Raine asked.

Christina lifted a shoulder. "We're not sure. Days. I doubt we even have a week."

"So we get him back. Hell, we go in today. We'll extract him from the damaged stone and tuck him safely away in another until we can find a host for him."

"Who will be the host?" Christina asked.

Liam shook his head. "I don't know. It would take an extraordinary human to be willing to merge with him. We were fortunate when we arrived in this dimension that the priest's visions had told him of our coming and he had found men and women willing to take on the burden."

"We'll find someone in this century," Dante said. "It may take a while, but he's been trapped for thousands of years. A few more will be only a blip."

Mal nodded agreement. "We will. If we have to scour the earth to do it. So that's essentially the plan. We'll touch base with the intermediary to negotiate acquisition of the brooch at any price before it's delivered to Folsom. If that doesn't pan out, we'll fall back on surveillance, pinpoint the location, and acquire it by less legitimate means."

Dante grinned. "You mean steal it."

"Of course."

Liam shifted so that he faced Dante more directly. "You're on point. We've learned that the intermediary is staying at the Algonquin Hotel."

"Fine," Dante said. What the hell. A new mission would keep his mind occupied. God knew he needed an escape from his memories and regrets. "What's his name? Have we got a dossier?"

"Her," Mal corrected with a quick glance toward Liam. "And we do."

Liam handed Dante a thin folder. He opened it—and found himself staring into the eyes of Brenna Hart.

The only women he'd ever loved.

The woman he could not have.

The woman who, he was certain, absolutely hated his guts.

Chapter 2

"Brenna! Oh my god, oh my god! Look at you!"

I bite back a grin that is equal parts amusement and embarrassment. Despite having just turned thirty-five, Whitney Green is bouncing like a teenager in the lobby of the famous Algonquin Hotel.

"Stand up! Stand up!"

Since there's really no battling Whitney when she is determined, I comply. She takes a step back and looks me up and down, her eyes narrowed in professional appraisal. "Brenna Hart, you are amazing. I swear you look just like you did at twenty-three."

I laugh. "You know I love you, Whitney, but you are such a liar."

"Don't even. You're gorgeous and you know it."

I don't, actually. Pretty, yes. Gorgeous, no. But I'm fine with that. In my work it pays to be able to blend. Glam it up if I need to mix with celebrities or politicians. Dress it down for the working-class folk. Minimal makeup and gray suits if I'm doing the corporate thing. I'm a human chameleon, and that works for me.

Today, I'm somewhere between glam and corporate. I've got that day-at-the-salon glow coupled with the tiger-in-the-boardroom mentality. I discovered long ago that it pays to know what my clients find both attractive and trustworthy. For Michael Folsom, that's competence coupled with a moneyed privilege.

No problem there; I can pull that off in spades.

In Folsom's case, it doesn't hurt that he wants to get me in bed. And I wasn't averse to using that knowledge to drive up my price. After all, any type of risk increases my fee; that's the nature of the business.

In his case, the job itself was reasonably easy—convince the daughter of an elderly earl to sell me a lovely Renaissance brooch rather than donating it to the British Museum. Honestly, she practically tripped over herself to accept my first offer on Michael's behalf.

But the fact that Michael very obviously wanted to celebrate after I pulled off the deal? Well, anything that tilts toward intimacy, my emotions, or starts to smell like sex is going to have me ratcheting those fees up.

I played fast and loose with my emotions once before and I'd lost big time. Now I keep my heart locked up tighter than most of the museums I work with. That's not to say I'm not open to sex—frankly, it's a sport I enjoy, and at thirty-six, I think I've developed a nice little toolbox of skills. But if I even smell a relationship, I take the next train to singles-ville with no regrets and no looking back.

Not that I explained any of that to Michael. I just caught the scent of interest and upped the price. No harm no foul, and the worst that could happen was that he walked. The best, my already happy bank account got another dose of glee.

In Michael's case, it was the latter. And, frankly, he wanted that brooch so much he would have paid a whole lot more.

As my mind has been wandering, Whitney has been chattering and leading us through the lobby toward the Blue Bar, the cozy watering hole inside the hotel. The space itself is narrow, with dim lighting highlighted by glowing blue fixtures scattered about and walls of drawings by Al Hirschfeld featuring all sorts of Broadway shows.

I especially love the whimsy of the sparkling lights set into the bar itself, and the Sinatra tunes that are pumped out through the sound system never fail to make me smile.

We take seats at the bar, order dirty martinis, and settle in to drink and catch up. We met in London when I was doing an internship at one of the premiere auction houses and she was trying to make it as a model. Now she lives in New York and owns a salon that is constantly booked solid with celebrities and socialites. I still live in London and work as a private acquisitions consultant. In other words, people hire me to get things for them.

It's an excellent, lucrative job with all sorts of benefits, not the least of which is traveling. And it's all the more fabulous because I invented the job myself, which means that I call all the shots, make all the decisions, take all the risks, and reap all the rewards.

My life more or less fell apart when I was twenty-three, and from my heartache spouted an epiphany. Now I rely only on myself, and I expect nothing from anyone else.

It makes for much less disappointment, that's for damn sure.

"—total brats," Whitney is saying, as we move along our conversational map. "He refused to discipline them. Just refused. And conversation? Good god, the man thought that talking about the television lineup was scintillating. I don't know how he earned the fortune he did."

"You told him to take a hike," I say.

"Eventually." She flashes the crooked smile I remember from our wild London days. "First I used him shamelessly. His cock was the best thing going for him."

I have just taken a sip of my martini, and it's all I can do not to spit it out when I laugh.

"You seeing anyone serious?" she asks me.

"Not even remotely."

She leans forward, her breath evidencing the three martinis we have each now had. "Speaking of you and your love life, do you remember the guy you dated when we lived in London?"

My heart does an unpleasant skittering thing. "You're kidding, right?" I dated only one man in London, and it was the most emotional, sensual, mind-blowing relationship of my life. It was also the relationship that ripped my heart out, stomped on it, kicked it to the curb, and had me swearing off men for over a year. Which on the whole was a good thing. After all, battery-powered boyfriends don't tell you they love you and then walk off into the sunset on the arm of another woman.

Now, of course, I have my new and improved fuck 'em and leave 'em approach to dating. But I still keep the vibrator in the top drawer of my bedside table.

Whitney has the decency to wince a bit, even as her cheeks turn pink. "Sorry. That was stupid. I mean, you don't forget the biggest asshole to ever warm your bed, right?"

I press my hand over hers and look her deep in the eyes. "Whitney, I love you. But you get no more martinis. I mean, why are we even talking about this?"

"What was his name?"

I really don't want to talk about this, but like the Energizer Bunny, Whitney will just keep going and going.

Besides, I can say his name without it hurting. It's been thirteen years. My wounds have healed and my scars have faded. And, frankly, he did me a favor. If not for him, I wouldn't have my job, my approach to life, any of it.

"Dante," I say. "Why?"

"Because I think he's behind you. Sitting at that table near the door."

Suddenly, it is very, very cold in here. And at the same time, it's very, very warm. Beads of sweat pop up at the base of my neck, and my underarms feel suddenly damp. Honestly, I'm having a little trouble breathing.

Not possible. Absolutely not possible.

I reach for my martini and take a long swallow. And then I take another.

"No way," I say, as the warm flush of alcohol hits my veins. "Why on earth would he be in New York?"

"You're in New York. I'm in New York."

"Yes, but—" Okay, actually, she has a point.

"Aren't you going to turn around?"

I remain perfectly still.

"Well?" Whitney demands.

"Give me a second. I'm thinking." Honestly, I know I shouldn't look. Dante Storm had swept into my life just as his name suggested. I'd been twenty-three at the time, awed and amazed that a man fifteen years older than me would be even remotely interested in a somewhat introverted girl who couldn't even make up her mind what canapé to choose, much less what to do with herself for the rest of her life.

We'd met at a party thrown by the owner of Dashiell's, an auction house on par with Christie's or Sotheby's. I was spending a year abroad, interning there while I tried to decide if I wanted to simply jump headfirst into life or go back to the States and finish my dissertation.

I suppose I was primed for a distraction, and Dante was a distraction times ten. Even now, I can feel the way my chest tightened and my pulse kicked up when he walked through the wide double doors, the black dinner jacket and slacks making him look like a man from another era. A man with dark blond hair swept back from his face in a way that highlighted his hypnotic, golden eyes. His wide shoulders looked as though they could bear the weight of the world, and something about his regal posture suggested that they did.

I'd never seen him before, and I knew he wasn't a regular at Dashiell's. Even so, he strode into the room like he owned it— and drew the attention of every person at the event, male and female, as he did.

How is it possible that I can barely remember the name of the guy I slept with last week, and yet I can recall everything about Dante. His scent, all spice and musk with just a hint of cinnamon. His touch, so deceptively gentle that when it turned rough it was all the more exciting. The scar that sliced from his shoulder down to his hipbone. A reminder, he'd called it. But I'd dubbed it a map and let my kisses follow it home.

And his tattoos. Five amazing, brilliantly colored birds in a cluster on his back. Phoenixes, he'd said.

He'd had a way of making me feel alive. Beautiful. Vibrant.

With Dante, I felt as though I was lit from the inside. At least until he'd snuffed that light out for good.

He'd hurt me, more than I'd ever been hurt before or since. And I absolutely, one-hundred percent have no interest in seeing him now.

Really.

Oh, hell.

I turn.

And the moment I do, I'm certain I've just made the biggest mistake of my life.

He hasn't changed. Not one iota. And I know that I must be seeing him through the eyes of my youth because he is fifteen years older than me, and fifty-one-year-old men do not look that hot. Even celebrities can't hold back Mother Nature the way that Dante can.

Except, dear god, he has. He is still perfection. Frankly, from my new thirty-something perspective, he's even more perfect than he was before. I'd been intrigued by his older-man persona, but now I'm simply drawn to his masculinity. He's a man, not a boy. And so help me, my pulse is pounding, my skin tingling in anticipation of his touch. And despite thirteen long years, it feels as though not a moment has passed, and the wild burn of our connection still courses through me.

A connection I crave but can no longer trust.

I swallow, realizing that those wild, golden eyes have been taking me in, and I know the man well enough to know that he has seen my reaction. My weakness.

I turn back to Whitney, certain that I am flushed.

More than that, certain that I am wet.

Fuck.

I close my hand over the clutch-style purse I'd put next to me on the bar. "I should run," I say. "I have a meeting in the morning. Sign it to my room, okay? And I'll call the spa tomorrow. We can plan on lunch before I go back."

"Oh, hell," she says. "I should have kept my mouth shut."

"No, really. It's okay. I just need to—" I cut myself off because I'm doing a terrible job of lying, but I really want to get out of here. I start to slide off the stool, but when I see Whitney's face—her tiny little wince—I know that I am completely and royally screwed.

Honestly, I don't know that I even needed to see her face. Because the moment I stop moving, I can feel him behind me. The heat of him. The way he upsets the fabric of the universe, so that the air around him seems to thrum, making my body suddenly hyperaware all over again.

Double fuck.

I draw a deep breath, then plaster on my corporate smile. I turn in the chair, planning to say something witty, though I haven't worked out exactly what that might be yet.

Or perhaps I'll just meet his eyes then walk away, letting him know in no uncertain terms that he is part of my past and needs to stay there.

In the end, I do none of those things.

I turn.

I see him.

And before I can stop myself, I pick up my martini and throw it in his face.

Chapter 3

I push past him, keeping my head down because looking at this man would be a very bad idea, and I don't stop until I reach the elevator bank.

Unfortunately for me, there are no elevators waiting, and my fantasy that I will be magically whisked away from him is only that—a fantasy.

In reality, he's walking straight toward me, his long strides eating up the ground between us. He is looking right at me, and he is moving with such bearing and confidence that for a moment I have to wonder if I imagined tossing a drink all over him.

But no, as he gets closer I see that his shirt is damp and his hair is slicked back, as if he's used the vodka as hair tonic.

"Not the greeting I'd hoped for," he says as he approaches. "But probably one I should have expected."

"You walked out on me, you bastard." I snap the words out, surprising myself. First I toss alcohol, then I verbally pounce. For a woman who prides herself on being icy calm in high-level negotiations, I am running seriously hot.

Apparently, that's what three dirty martinis in under an hour will do to a girl.

"Yes," he says. "I did."

His easy acknowledgment doesn't smooth my ruffled feathers

in the least. "Not only that, but you walked away from me on the arm of another woman."

At that, I think I see something like pain flash in his eyes. But he offers no rebuttal or explanation. He simply says, "It's been a long time, Brenna. And I didn't come to talk about the past."

I *didn't come.*

Well, that answers the question I'd been too ruffled to even raise in my own mind: This wasn't a chance encounter, this was a full-blown surprise attack.

"You prick," I say. "You had to know how seeing you would upset me. You couldn't have called me? Called the hotel? Had the bellboy deliver a message while you waited in the lobby."

"I'm sorry I hurt you. Truly. I can't even begin to tell you how sorry I am. But I have a job for you, and time is of the essence, and—"

"You know what, Dante? Just shut the fuck up."

His eyes actually widen and I silently applaud myself. I have balls of steel in business, but I've never put up much of a fight where my personal life is concerned. I tell myself that I have the alcohol to thank, but a tiny, secret part of me knows that's not the truth—the truth is that I haven't much cared about my personal life for the last thirteen years.

I rush on before my nerve or my buzz fades. "I thought we had something real. *Six months.* Christ, Dante, I was ready to marry you and have your babies. I loved you so much it fucking terrified me. And now all you say is that you're sorry you hurt me? Well, guess what, Dante. I am over you. I am so over you it isn't even funny. And you know what else? Fuck you."

I spit the last two words at him, and while I should storm off, the elevator has come and gone during my tirade and there is no place to which I can storm.

Not only that, those last two words are hanging between us in giant cartoon letters in pulsating purple neon. And as I watch him watching me, a single, horrible, wonderful thought rises within me, and as much as I want to tamp it back, I can't seem to make it go away.

Fuck you.

Fuck you, Dante.

Fuck. Me.

Oh, dear god, I must be going insane, but in that moment, I want him in my bed. I want to fuck him out of my system. I want to prove to myself that the fact that I haven't been able to get him out of my head for thirteen freaking years is because I was young and relatively inexperienced. But I'm not anymore, and one more go between the sheets will prove that he's nothing special. And maybe—*maybe*—I can move on instead of feeling the way I feel now.

Which is that I want him to touch me.

Which is pathetic after so damn long. But, dammit, I can't seem to erase the thought from my head.

Dante, thank goodness, doesn't seem to be able to read my mind. "I can say I'm sorry as many times as you want me to," he says, "but when I'm done I'll still need your help." He takes a step toward me, and once again I can feel the universe shift and bubble. The air is thick and I'm having a little trouble breathing. I try to stand perfectly still because I don't want him to see the effect he is having on me. For that matter, I don't want to be affected.

So much for wishes and wants...

"This is hard for me, too, Brenna," and there is such heated longing in his voice that I almost believe him. But I know damn well that he doesn't want me anymore. He's the one who walked away. I frown and rub my temples, sure that I am hearing an emotion that really isn't there.

"But this is important," he continues. "You acquired a piece recently for a client. I need to acquire it from you."

I know what piece he's talking about, of course. I charge a significant amount for my services, which means that I have the luxury of taking off between jobs. Since I've had only one job in the last four months, I know that he is talking about Folsom's brooch.

"I'm afraid that's not possible. Even if I were inclined to screw over my client and sell it to you instead of him, I don't have it. I delivered the brooch about two hours ago. Right in that bar."

If the news fazes Dante, he doesn't show it. I remember that he'd worked in private security and that his emotions had always been hard to read. He was skilled at hiding them—except when we were alone and he was unguarded.

Or, at least, I'd always believed in the honesty of those unguarded moments in bed. But knowing what I know now—that he'd dumped me at the drop of a hat and left the country with another woman with no warning whatsoever—I have to wonder if those moments weren't an act. Some sort of fantasy designed to make me believe he loved me.

But why?

What the hell was the point, other than to torture me?

For a long moment he stays silent. Then he says, "You misunderstand. We want to hire you to acquire it. Or, at least, to smooth the way for us to arrange our own acquisition."

I cross my arms over my chest. "I see." I speak slowly, figuring I need time to gather my courage. But I've drunk three glasses of liquid courage already and have bolstered that with thirteen years' worth of anger. So there's not much gathering to do. On the contrary, I'm more like a roller coaster, making the slow climb to a dropping off point, and when I go over, there'll be no stopping me.

I step toward him, and as I do I feel that frisson of desire, that slice of need. I remember the touch of his hands upon my breasts, the feel of his lips upon my skin. I hear the sweet words he whispered. Promises of eternity, of forever, of a love that would last through time.

And that is the final push—I go over and down, hurtling

toward a solution that will either kill me or save me, but at this point there is no getting off the ride.

"I don't want your money, Dante. I want you in my bed. I've had you in my head for thirteen years, and I just want to move on. One last fuck, Dante, and then it's over. Give me that, and I'll see if I can't reacquire that damn brooch for you."

I keep business cards in the front pocket of my purse, and I tuck one now into the breast pocket of his tailored suit. "My cell number's on the card," I say. "Let me know what you decide."

Then—because finally the fates are in my favor—the elevator doors slide open and I slip inside.

But as the doors are closing, Dante thrusts his hand in, triggering the safety mechanism. The doors slide open again and he bursts inside, his eyes flaring with a violent heat. He's in front of me in an instant, his arms caging me, and my back is pressed against the wall so that the handrail digs painfully into my lower back. I welcome it, though, because—*oh, god, yes*—this is the kind of primal heat I am craving. The wild, violent claiming that will melt away all the hard edges I've built up over the years.

This is what I want. What I need.

This is what will destroy me, but as his mouth crushes against mine, I really don't care. In fact, I can manage only one coherent thought.

Surrender.

And so I do.

* * * *

Dear god, he'd missed this.

The touch of her. The feel of her. That fiery temper and her no-nonsense approach to life.

Being with her when she was twenty-three had been like embracing a lightning bolt, wild and vibrant, but just a little bit unfocused. Now, though, she was like the phoenix fire. Brilliant and bold and full of a magical heat that had the power to both reduce him to ashes and bring him back to life.

And oh, Christ but she was responsive. She'd been stiff at first, her body frozen with surprise by his unexpected assault. But she had soon melted under his touch, her mouth opening to him. Letting him tease and taste even as she did the same, her tongue working a kind of magic that was spreading through him, making his skin heat and his cock grow so goddamn hard that all he could think about was her words, her offer. *One last fuck.*

No. Dammit, he knew better. He couldn't go there. No matter how much he might still crave her, the idea of sinking his cock into her sweet, wet heat belonged safely in the realm of fantasy.

It had killed him once to let her go.

He wouldn't survive doing it twice.

Except this wasn't about him. This was about Merrick. Trapped. Dying.

This was about how far he would go to save a friend.

And, yes, this was about wanting her touch, even at the cost of his sanity.

Right now, that sanity was hanging by a thread. She was pressed against him, her breasts just as firm as he remembered, her nipples so tight he could feel the nubs through the thin material of her shirt and bra. One of her hands was on his shoulder, giving her leverage to rise up on her toes and kiss him, and oh, god, oh damn, all he wanted to do was yank up her skirt and fuck her hard, right here, right now, to hell with the security cameras and all the rest of that bullshit.

He pushed away, breaking the kiss roughly, a bit unsettled by the potency of his need.

She was breathing hard, her pale skin flushed. She reached up and dragged her fingers through her shoulder-length brown hair. It hung in waves to her shoulders, shorter than it had been in London, but the look was flattering. It accentuated those sharp cheekbones and drew the focus to her gunmetal gray eyes.

"Is that a yes?" Her voice was breathy, and he knew if he agreed they'd go to her room right now and not come out until morning.

That was just too goddamned tempting.

"I want to," he admitted, as her eyes dipped toward his crotch where his erection was even now tenting the slacks he'd worn.

When she looked up, he met her eyes unapologetically. "I want to very much."

She licked her lips, then nodded, as if conceding some unspoken contest.

"But only on the terms you set," he continued. He drew in a breath because this was the part he didn't want to say, but knew that he had to. "Because I will walk away again. So think long and hard about what you want. I hurt you once. I don't relish the idea of doing it again."

"I told you what I want." Her voice was cold now, without a trace of the heat he'd just felt in her touch. "You don't have to worry about me. I'm not going to get a taste of your magical cock and then fall head over heels for you again. I'm not twenty-three anymore, and I no longer believe in fairy tales. At least not the kind that come with happy endings."

Her words twisted inside him because he knew damn well he was the one who stole that from her. But before he could think what to say, she continued.

"I told you the truth, Dante. All I want is a fuck." She met his eyes, hers as hard as steel. "I don't want you."

He didn't flinch, even though her words cut him more than he had anticipated. "All right," he said. "But I want you to think about it, anyway. You can have your fee—whatever amount you want—or you can have me. Tell me tomorrow morning. Money or me." He drew out a business card of his own, this one with his home address. "I'll expect you by eight. Time is of the essence, baby."

"Maybe I don't want the job at all," she said.

"You want it," he said. And when the elevator doors opened again on her floor, he slipped out. Then he walked down the hall to the stairwell, not bothering to look back. He didn't need to; he knew that she was watching him go.

* * * *

Are you still in the bar?

My room in the Algonquin is small, and it takes little time for me to pace the length of it and back again. I've done three laps before Whitney answers my text.

I am. After that show, I had to have another drink. So? Tell????

I start to give her my room number and tell her to come on up, but honestly, I need another drink, too. I may have been humming on three martinis, but Dante burned them right out of my system.

Order me a dirty martini. I'll be down in five.

I arrive right as the martini does, and I take a long swallow even before climbing onto the barstool. Then I take another five minutes to explain what he needs and what I offered.

Then I have to wait three more minutes for her to quit laughing and high-fiving me. Apparently, I have just become a role model to women everywhere.

Except I don't much feel like a role model. Now that the alcohol has mostly faded from my veins, I feel just the opposite, actually. I feel a bit like an idiot.

"This is stupid," I say. "I say over and over that he won't break my heart, but that's a lie. Or maybe it's not. Because how do you break something that's already shattered?"

I put my elbows on the bar and bury my head in my hands. "I'm pathetic, you know. Thirteen years, and he can still wound me."

"Which begs the question of why you propositioned the guy," Whitney says, then cringes when I lift my head and scowl at her.

"Okay, the reason he can still hurt you is because you loved him. You thought you were going to ride off into the sunset together." She shrugs. "Simple as that."

Which, of course, isn't simple at all.

"It scared me," I admit. "What he and I had. Did I tell you that back then? That it really, really terrified me."

She shakes her head. "No, but I get that. He was older and settled in a career and you were just starting out."

"True, but it was more than that. I felt—I don't know, I guess I felt so alive, so *right* that I didn't trust it. I mean, I was just this normal girl from a normal life. How could I suddenly be in the middle of this epic love? I was afraid it was all going to be ripped away."

She rolled her eyes. "You always did over-analyze everything. You should have told me. I would have smacked some sense into you."

"Except I was right," I say, and she makes a face.

"Not because you were normal. It didn't work because he was an asshole. Not because you didn't deserve him."

But I'm not really listening anymore. "I tested it on my own." I half-smile, remembering my own stupidity. "Remember Rob? The guy who worked at that museum in Prague? He took me out to dinner one night, and I could tell he was interested, and I just wanted to know—"

"You slept with him? Oh my god, Brenna!"

"No! I just—I just let him kiss me. I guess I wanted to see if it would sweep me away the way Dante's kisses did."

"Did it?"

I shake my head. "Not at all. And afterward, all I could think of was how horrible I was because Dante was my everything."

I stifle a shudder as I remember the rest. Because less than a week later, Dante walked away. And even though it's foolish, ever since, I've felt like I broke a spell that day. Or that I brought on a curse.

Either way, somehow I screwed up my happily ever after.

And that's the real reason I don't believe in fairy tales anymore. They're too damn fragile.

Chapter 4

He really was a goddamn fool.

Dante paced the length of his first floor den, from fireplace to wet bar and then back again as the morning sun streamed in through the front windows. He'd bought the brownstone almost two centuries ago when it had come on the market, sold by an industrialist who'd climbed too high, too fast and had spent his great fortune on wine, women, and food, apparently thinking that those sweet perks of the nascent modern age would never fade.

They had faded, though, at least for him. And Dante had stepped in to pick up the pieces.

He loved the building—five stories, each carefully decorated over the years with pieces that he had painstakingly sought to acquire. When one lived forever, there was no need to hurry, and Dante had taken his time making this home.

The only thing it lacked was a companion.

Fuck.

He paused in front of the wet bar and talked himself out of pouring a drink. It was still a quarter to eight in the morning, and he ought to observe at least one or two proprieties.

But damned if he didn't want the buzz. Because Brenna would be here soon, and goddamn him all to hell, he really didn't know what he wanted her answer to be.

He wanted her. Dear god, he wanted her. Had been wanting her—missing her for thirteen long years.

But to have her now would only bring heartache to both of them because it couldn't last. All that the future could hold for them was for her to grow old in his arms. For her to suffer as her body shifted and changed and finally failed, while he stayed young and strong. Constant. Unchanging. Except for the added pain in his heart as he went through the rest of eternity knowing that he had held perfection only to watch it fade in the blink of an eye.

There was no escaping that inevitability. As much as he might wish it otherwise, he could not shed his immortality as a snake sheds its skin.

During his darkest times, he craved the abyss of death. He was so lonely. But that was a relatively new sensation—one that he had not experienced before he met Brenna.

Before her, he had been content to live out his days in the company of as many women as were willing to share his bed. He told himself he enjoyed the variety of which his brothers who were mated could no longer partake. For thousands of years, he had lived that way and had told himself he was living the good life.

Then he'd met her—a dark-haired girl with a quick wit and a lithe body. A girl with gunmetal gray eyes that seemed to see right through him—and that silently called him a liar.

Because he was, dammit. It wasn't variety he wanted, it was her. Miraculously, she had wanted him, too.

They had fallen headfirst together into love, their days filled with laughter, their nights with passion. She had told him her dreams, her ambitions. He had shared his work, his passions, his stories.

He had longed for the day when it would feel right to also share his secrets, but he hadn't rushed. He had believed in his heart that such a day was coming, and that his astounding revelation would not shake her to the core.

Like a fool, he had believed that she was his one, his mate, his true match. That he could keep her by his side for all eternity.

He had believed that the depth of her feelings matched the depth of his own.

But then he had seen her in the arms of another man, and he was struck hard by the painful realization that what he had believed she felt was only an illusion. He did not doubt that she cared for him, but he knew that she could not be truly his. And no matter how much he had hoped and believed otherwise, she could not share eternity with him.

She was mortal—and he could not make it otherwise. Because the phoenix fire could only bring immortality to a true mate, a timeless passion. Anything less, and the fire would do what fire does best—it would burn, but not restore.

Dante knew of only eight women who braved the phoenix fire over the millennia. Each had professed a heart overflowing with love and passion. With a pure, timeless longing.

Seven had been reduced to dust, their deaths breaking the hearts of the brothers who had loved them dearly.

Only one woman had stepped from the flame unscathed, a fresh tattoo of a phoenix marking her shoulder as a sign of both immortality and the challenge that she had faced and won.

Once, Dante had believed that Brenna could survive the flame, though he was never certain if he could actually ask her to risk it. Because if he was wrong, he did not think he could stand the horror of knowing the woman he loved had burned because of him.

But after he saw her in the arms of another man, that hesitation became moot. She was not his mate, and he would not stay.

Now, seeing her again, it had brought back both the passion and the pain.

He wanted her in his arms again. Wanted to taste her. Wanted to bend her to his will and make her groan. He wanted to take her to the heights of passion—to punish her with pleasure. To let her know just how much she had given up by not loving him the way he loved her.

Was he really that much of an asshole?

Yeah, he thought. *He was.*

Frustrated, he ran his fingers through his hair. He should never have taunted her. He should have simply said no. That he'd write her a check, but he wouldn't trade sex for commerce.

What would be even smarter would be to walk away from her permanently and get the brooch some other way. But he'd texted Liam and Mal after leaving the Algonquin last night, and Mal had one of the brothers in the Parisian office contact Folsom directly and offer to buy the brooch.

Folsom had turned him down flat, despite a truly obscene offer. "I have more money than I know what to do with," Folsom had said. "Now I indulge my passions."

A little more digging had turned up the unsurprising fact that Brenna was one of his passions. He'd taken her to dinner twice over the last month, and according to his personal assistant—who needed extra cash to help out her drug-addicted sister—he had made a number of calls to her on the pretense of discussing the acquisition, but which had really seemed designed for no purpose other than to hear her voice.

Dante could hardly fault the man for that.

Dante also knew that Brenna had turned down Folsom's efforts to get her into his bed, presumably because that would strain their professional relationship. What he didn't know was if she would slide between the sheets now that their business arrangement had come to a close.

The thought roiled in his stomach, and the taste of jealousy sat bitter on his tongue.

He was about to rethink his decision not to have a shot of scotch this early when his door chimed.

For a moment, he just stood there. Then he shook himself,

feeling like an ass. No, more like a thirteen-year-old boy. Not that he had ever actually been a thirteen-year-old boy...

Frustrated with himself, he went to the door and pulled it open. She stood there, her loose hair framing her lovely face, and all he wanted to do was take her into his arms and hold her.

Get a fucking grip.

He ordered himself to step back, to hold the door open for her. Each step thought out and executed, just as if she was a mission.

Because he damn sure couldn't treat her like most of the women who crossed his threshold.

Women he took. Women he claimed.

Women who melted with pleasure at his touch, and then went on their way when the next day's sun rose in the east.

He might want her in his arms, but hadn't he already lectured himself that it would be a bad idea? Because if he had her again, he knew damn well that he wouldn't want her to leave in the morning.

Cash. She needed to choose cash. It was the best way to keep her from getting hurt again.

As for him?

Nothing was going to heal his hurt. Nothing but time. And god knew he had an eternity of that.

He realized she was still standing in the doorway, eyeing him with curiosity. "You can come on in," he said, gesturing to the living area that opened off the foyer.

She shoved her hands into the pockets of her sundress. The action tugged the material down, making it pull taut against her breasts. He could see the outline of her nipples, and he felt his cock twitch.

Christ, he was a mess. He'd spent three millennia walking this earth. He'd fought in wars. He'd dined with kings. He'd hobnobbed with men and women whose names now filled history books.

How was it that this one woman shattered his senses?

Since he needed to move, he turned away from her as if to lead the way, but the brush of her fingers on his sleeve had him turning back. Had him swallowing a groan simply from the reaction that innocent touch had elicited.

"Wait." Her voice was soft, and he saw that she was biting her lower lip. "I—I should apologize for yesterday. My—ah, the price I quoted was unprofessional. I was a little drunk and a lot pissed. Or maybe vice-versa. At any rate, I was being foolish." She drew in a breath, then managed a smile. "I'll take the job. I'll take it for cash."

He told himself it was relief that had him reeling. Too bad he knew that was a lie.

She dragged her fingers through her hair, mussing it and making him remember how she looked in bed after a long night of making love.

He forced himself to look down.

"You messed me up a long time ago, Dante." Her voice was soft but firm. "But I'm a grown woman now, and although I am quite certain that having you back in my bed would be exciting and wonderful, it was stupid of me to suggest it. Stupid and vindictive and—" She halted, and something about the way her breath hitched had him looking up. "—and dangerous," she finished.

"Dangerous?"

She shrugged, her eyes aimed somewhere over his left shoulder.

"Look at me." He kept his voice low. Commanding.

She looked, and he saw a desire reflected back at him that equaled his own.

"Tell me what you mean." He knew he should drop it. This is what he wanted—cold, hard cash, and nothing personal between them. Didn't matter. He took a step toward her anyway, and as he did, the heat between them built. A heat sufficient to burn away all his good sense. "Tell me why it would be dangerous."

"Don't." The word was strained. Full of a plea. Full of pain.

And he cursed himself silently for being an ass. For being confused. For wanting her. For knowing he couldn't have her. And for letting his cock do the thinking instead of his head.

"Sorry. Right. Cash it is." He took a step back in order to allow more oxygen to his brain. "My office is next door. Come on. We'll go cut you a check."

"I prefer a wire transfer," she said, but she fell in step beside him. He was reaching for the doorknob when he realized that she'd stopped. He turned, then cringed when he saw her looking at the original Monet hanging by his front door.

"I acquired that painting. It was one of my first jobs when I went out on my own."

He knew that, of course. Hadn't he watched her career for five solid years? He'd probably still be watching it if Liam and Mal hadn't convinced him that he was sinking into a dangerous quicksand, and just might be crossing the line into stalker-ville, too.

"I wanted the Monet," he said, struggling to reveal nothing in his voice. The painting revealed enough. "You had the ability to acquire it."

"Why didn't you tell me that you're PB Enterprises?"

Because PB Enterprises doesn't exist. Because I only acquired the painting because we'd seen it together one afternoon at the British Museum. Because I felt like a fool wanting you so desperately and knowing that you didn't want me. Not fully. Not completely.

Not enough to last through eternity.

He said none of that. Instead, he said flatly, "It didn't seem important."

"Oh." She swallowed. "No, why would it be?" The smile that touched her lips seemed fake. "We should probably get to your office."

She started toward the door, and he knew that the moment

she went through it, his opportunity would be lost. It would be a cash-only transaction. Hands off. Purely business.

Just as it should be.

Oh, fuck it.

He grabbed her, then pulled her toward him with such a wild, violent motion that she stumbled against him and had to cling to his shoulders to steady herself, breathing hard.

"Why?" he growled.

"Why what?"

"You don't need the money. Why take cash? Why not take me?"

Her breath shuddered, and he caught the minty scent of toothpaste. He didn't just want the scent—he wanted the taste.

"I told you. I was being stupid. Angry. Unprofessional."

"That's not it."

She struggled in his arms; he tightened them.

"Dammit, Dante, let me go."

"Tell me the truth."

Her gray eyes flashed. "Maybe I just don't want you."

"The hell you don't. You're wet right now, and we both know it. You're as wet as I am hard. And baby, I'm very, very hard."

He could feel her pulse kick up. He saw her pupils dilate and her skin flush. Her lips parted.

Every inch of her body screamed the truth of his words. But with her mouth, she said only, "Bullshit."

He stroked his hand slowly up her back as his other hand cupped her ass. He couldn't be sure, but he thought she was biting the inside of her cheek. "Fair enough," he said. "Maybe you're just scared."

"Very little scares me," she retorted. "Least of all you."

"Really? Well, that makes only one of us. Because baby, you scare me to death. One look and you can melt me. One kiss and you could destroy me."

"Then why not just let me go?" She asked the question

plaintively, but the breathiness of her voice told a different story. And so did her body. She'd moved closer. Just barely, but he could tell. Her chest was crushed against his, and he could feel her pebble-hard nipples brush against him.

"Just give me the money." Now he heard the plea. "Walk away and be done with me just like you did before."

"I should," he admitted. His throat was raw. "I really should. But I'm just so goddamned hungry."

Chapter 5

"Hungry?"

I ask the question as if I don't understand what he means. But I do. Oh, dear god, I do. Being in his arms feels like coming home, and though I know that I am making a mistake, I cannot help myself. Hell, I don't want to help myself.

I surrender to him.

But at the same time, I claim him, too. His mouth. His body. My fingers twine in his hair, remembering the sensual feel of those silky strands. My tongue wars with his, demanding and taking. And when he slides one hand up between our bodies to cup my breast, I moan against his mouth, then grind my pelvis against him.

"Harder," I demand when he teases my nipple between his fingers.

He pulls back, his eyes searching mine.

"You know what I like," I whisper. "I know you remember."

"I remember everything about you," he agrees. "The way you tremble when I stroke my tongue along the curve of your ear. The way your breath shudders when I kiss my way down your belly. The way you cry out when you come." He nips my lower lip, making me squirm. "And I remember that you rarely asked for what you wanted."

"I was young and naïve. I'm a woman now, Dante. A lot of things have changed." I meet his eyes, and I know that mine must be a bit hesitant. Because there's no denying that my body has changed. That when he peels off this dress he will not see the tight, taut body of a girl in her early twenties with a Pilates addiction. Instead, he'll see the body of a thirty-six-year-old woman. Still in good shape, yes, thanks to those same Pilates and a personal trainer with a scary disposition. But nature is a bitch and you can only fight her so hard.

Then again, Dante seems to have figured out how to do that. My hands are all over him, and he is as tight and firm as I remember. There are no new lines on his face, no signs that life has treated him badly, or even that it has treated him at all. It is as if he is living on another plane, and those of us who are mere mortals are passing by beneath, moving down the conveyor of aging while he moves on the slower track ten stories above.

I won't deny that the hard perfection of his body is a delicious turn-on, but at the same time it makes me even more self-conscious.

I realize that I have looked away, lost in my thoughts and maybe even lost in a bit of self-pity. I am still in his arms, but the wildness has faded. Instead, he is looking at me so tenderly it makes me want to cry.

"I never thought you could be more beautiful," he says. "I was wrong. You're exceptional, Brenna. Your confidence. Your poise. Your fire. It shines in you. You have a strength now that you didn't have before, and baby, it's sexy as hell."

I manage a crooked smile. "You always did know how to say the right things."

"I like that you know how to say what you want."

"Do you?" I hear the challenge in his words.

"Tell me what you want, Brenna. Tell me every little thing."

My breath is coming hard, my nipples so tight it is painful. This is not a game I usually play. It's one thing to tell a man to touch you harder or faster. It's another thing entirely to direct the action. Especially when all I want to do is submit.

"I want you to touch me, Dante." I meet his eyes, my breath coming hard. "I want you to take me. Hard. Fast. I don't want to think. I just want to feel."

I watch the effect of my words play across his face. Confusion at first, and then a growing desire. And then—oh, god, and then—

He grabs my shoulders, then slams me back against the door. His mouth covers mine, hard and hot. Not a kiss so much as a sex, his tongue demanding entrance, warring with mine, taking and claiming and making me so goddamn wet that my panties are soaked and I can feel the slickness on my thighs.

I'm wearing a summer sundress, and as his tongue fucks my mouth, his hand fondles my breast, hard the way I like it, with his fingers teasing my nipple. I groan, then gasp when I realize that his other hand is sliding up my bare thigh to thrust inside my now soaked panties.

"Christ," he says, as he thrusts his fingers inside me. "You're so fucking wet."

I cry out in pleasure at the invasion, but he swallows the sound then breaks the kiss, his eyes studying my face as he fingerfucks me hard against the door.

"Is this what you wanted?" he asks, his voice a low growl of pleasure and demand.

"Yes." I can barely make the sound. I am too lost in pleasure. Too lost in the feel of him.

"No," he says. "More."

And before I can even process what he means, he has flipped me around so that I'm facing the wall, and he has thrust my dress up so that it's bundled around my waist.

"I'm going to fuck you, baby. I don't have a condom, but I'm clean. I have to have you—Christ, I think I'll die if I don't get inside you soon—but if you want me to stop, now's the time."

I say nothing. I just spread my legs and lean forward. I want this. Right now, I can think of nothing else I want more. Not even to breathe.

With one hand, he clutches my breast, holding me in place even as he ratchets up my arousal with the thumb that flicks roughly over my nipple. With his other, he yanks down my panties until they are stretched tight across my thighs, then even tighter when he orders me to spread my legs. I do, and his hand strokes me, his fingers teasing my core, thrusting inside me, taking what he wants and making me tremble with longing in the process.

He makes a sound that is somewhere between a sigh and a groan, and then I hear the wonderful, delicious, dangerous sound of his zipper easing down. I feel the head of his cock against my ass, and then the hard press of it against my core. He starts slow, easing inside me, and it is as if he is deliberately teasing me. Because I want it hard. Dammit, I want to be fucked.

I realize that he wants me to say it. To demand it. And I want it bad enough that I am not going to be shy—not now. Not with him.

"Harder," I beg. "Please, Dante, please, fuck me harder."

"Baby—" The endearment is ripped from him, and he slams into me, his body thrusting against mine, skin on skin, slick and intimate and wonderful.

He takes his hand off my breast so that he can hold me steady around my waist. Then with his other hand he reaches around to stroke my clit until I am little more than a mass of pleasure, so sweet and intense and wild and wonderful that it's a miracle I can even hold onto consciousness.

He bends forward, his body covering mine, his lips brushing the back of my neck, the curve of my ear, and that is when I lose it. Electric tremors shoot through me like lighting bolts converging at my cunt, and my muscles squeeze him, convulsions of pleasure that milk him until he cries out, the sound raw against my ear, and his arms tighten around me, pulling me close to him before we both sink to the ground.

"Holy crap," I say. I'm curled against him, my back against his chest, my dress still bunched around my waist.

He brushes my shoulder with a kiss and holds me close for a few moments before getting up. "Stay," he says softly, then returns a moment later with a warm, damp cloth.

He tugs my panties off, then gently cleans me. I meet his eyes, a little undone by the tenderness of this moment.

When he holds out a hand to help me up, I take it. "I need my panties," I say, holding out my hand.

He shakes his head. "I don't think so," he says. He tucks them in his pocket. I smirk as I adjust my dress.

I look at him. Just look at him. At the warmth in his eyes. The lines of his face. The strength in his body.

And the tenderness at the core of him.

I fell in love with him once—and I'm honestly not sure that I ever fell out of love.

But I do know one thing for sure—Dante Storm is dangerous to my heart. And whatever we started just now is something that we can't finish.

I meet his eyes and am about to say just that when he shakes his head. "No. Don't say it. You don't need to say it."

"What?"

"That we can't do it again."

"We can't."

"I know."

I stand in silence. I know why I can't; it's because he will break my heart.

But I don't know why he doesn't want me. I only know that he doesn't. I only know that he walked away once, and that he has already told me he will walk away again.

That should be enough, but then I have to go and open my mouth. I have to ask— "Why? Why did you leave?"

For a minute, I don't think that he's going to answer. But he surprises me by saying, "Because I was looking at forever."

"And you don't think I was, too?" I'm baffled. With Dante, forever was my mantra.

He looks at me, his eyes so sad I want to cry. "No," he says, "I know you weren't."

I start to protest, but he just shakes his head, like a dog shaking off water. "Let's go transfer your money."

"No," I say, standing firm.

He cocks his head, then winces. "We shouldn't have done this. It won't happen again. But please don't back out. I really need your help. I can't tell you how urgent this is."

"I'll help," I say. "But I don't want your money. And I don't want sex." That's not entirely true. I want it; I don't think I can handle it.

"Then why?"

"I don't know," I say. "Maybe because I loved you once upon a time."

Maybe because I still do.

* * * *

Dante leads me through the first floor of his brownstone to a sunroom that opens up onto a courtyard. That courtyard connects to another brownstone, and it is into that building that we enter. "The front is a private club—scotch and cigars, jazz and conversation," he says. "Dark Pleasures."

"I've heard of it," I admit. "It has a reputation for being both excellent and exclusive. You're a member?"

"One of the owners," he says. He looks at me. "I have been for a very long time."

"Even when you lived in London?"

"Even then."

I nod, taking in the simple fact that I don't know this man as well as I had thought. I think that is what he is trying to show me in his not so subtle way. But it doesn't matter. I know the core of him. I've known that since the first moment I looked into his eyes when he brought me a glass of wine and told me I looked like sunshine. I've known it since our first meal when he brushed a dab of ketchup from the corner of my mouth and I shivered all the way down to my toes. I think I've known it since our first touch, our first kiss.

I exhale, forcing myself to shake off my melancholy as I follow him to an old-fashioned elevator with a cage-style door. We step in, then rise to the third floor, the gears creaking as we move. "The club takes up the first and second floors," he says. But the third is office space, for both the club and Phoenix Security."

I nod. *That* job I remember. "You're still with the company?"

His grin is almost a smirk. "I think it's fair to say that I'm a lifer."

I cock my head. "You own that company as well?"

"A piece of it, anyway."

He points to the floors above us as the elevator slows to a stop. "Four is reserved for guests. Five is my friend Raine's private apartment. Odds are good he'll be at the meeting."

I nod, trying to remember it all. I'm not sure why it matters, though. He's sharing life trivia when he has already made it clear he has no interest in sharing a life.

I follow him down a balcony-style hallway that overlooks what obviously used to be the grand ballroom in this converted brownstone. The last door is polished oak, and it has a brass placard identifying it as the office of Phoenix Security.

We enter and step into a classy, polished reception area. A dark-haired man with a lean, bad-boy appearance, who looks like he could be Hollywood's new hot thing, steps in from a door on the far side. He's wearing jeans and a black T-shirt with a white phoenix embroidered on the breast pocket. "You must be Brenna.

I'm Malcolm Greer." He steps forward and I shake his hand. "Glad you're helping us out."

"Happy to," I say, glancing sideways at Dante.

"Mal is one of the company presidents," Dante says. "With Liam," he adds, pointing to a linebacker-sized man with a wide smile and serious eyes. "And Raine's just along for the ride." The third man has close-cropped hair and sleeves of tats that disappear under a T-shirt similar to the black one worn by his friends.

Dante formally introduces me, we do the meet and greet thing, and I follow the men into a conference room. Honestly, it's like being in a pressure cooker of hotness laced with a helping of testosterone.

"Dante explained what we need?" Mal asks.

"The brooch," I say. "Though I have no idea why there's so much urgency."

"I'm afraid that's harder to explain," Liam says. "And you'll forgive me if I don't try. It's not actually necessary for what we're hiring you to do."

I lean back in my chair, not bothering to correct him. I'm not really being hired. I was well-fucked, and this is now a freebie. Frankly, that's not something I feel the need to share. "Why me? Why don't one of you call him? Make him an offer he can't refuse."

"We tried that already, Ms. Hart," Raine says. "Got shot down."

"Really?" I frown. My experience with Michael is that he's very interested in his bottom line. "Did he say why?"

"He said that he's a collector of cursed artifacts," Liam said, "and that this isn't about the money."

Beside me, Dante shifts. "When did he say that? The report I read simply indicated that he wasn't interested in parting with the piece."

"You read the e-mail report. The secure communication came

about half an hour later. Cursed," Liam repeats as if that word holds special import. And from the way Dante leans forward, his forehead creased into a frown, I guess that it does.

"I do a lot of research on every item I try to acquire," I say. "I assure you, this one has no history of a curse." I glance at each of them in turn. "So what is that code for?"

Mal glances at Dante and smiles. I have the oddest feeling that it's a smile of approval.

"We need you to gain access to Mr. Folsom's house. We need you to talk with him. We need you to learn the location of the brooch—presumably it's in a safe, and presumably Folsom has several safes on site. And that, Ms. Hart, is all that we need. We'll wire you so that we can see what you see. It will help us to map the location after the fact."

I look at all of them in turn. "You're going to *steal* it?"

"Yeah," Dante says. "We're going to steal it."

"But—"

He closes his hand over mine, and when he looks in my eyes I feel that delicious little quiver. "Just temporarily. We'll return it almost immediately. Intact."

I lift a brow, but nothing I can think of to say seems quite sarcastic or cutting enough.

"Please, Brenna," he says. "I need you to trust me."

And—against all reason and better judgment—I do.

Chapter 6

I am thinking that perhaps I should have paid more attention to my reason and better judgment as I stride over the threshold and into Michael Folsom's swank penthouse apartment. It takes up the top three stories of the Xavier Building, one of the city's most sought after addresses on Fifth Avenue. Folsom no longer owns the building, but he used to. When he sold it, he retained ownership of the top three floors and had them converted into one residence.

Rumor has it that he spent more on the conversion and remodel than he received for the sale of the entire remaining building. Until now, I thought that was a ridiculous urban legend. But looking around at this incredible interior with its elegant finish, attention to detail, and high-quality furnishings, I think the story might actually be true.

"I'm so glad you called," he says, taking my hand and pressing a gentlemanly kiss to my fingertips. "I was beginning to feel snubbed."

I laugh lightly. "You've retained me enough times to know that I don't mix business with pleasure."

"You're not currently working for me." The heat in his voice is obvious. So is the invitation.

On any normal day, I would shut this down right now.

But this is not a normal day.

I lick my lips, conjure a smile, and wonder what Dante is thinking at this very moment. Because he is seeing and hearing everything.

And for some reason, that makes me want to kick the show up into high gear.

I take a single step toward Folsom. "No," I say huskily. "I'm not."

I see the reflection of my reply on his face immediately. A man who not only wants a woman, but expects to get her.

The truth is, under other circumstances I might actually be interested. Michael Folsom isn't my type, but there's no denying that he's attractive. He has soft, almost boyish features. A sort of Leonardo DiCaprio vibe that doesn't usually do it for me, but I've seen plenty of evidence of other women's interest. And the fact is, just a man's interest can be a turn-on, and Folsom has never made his a secret.

If he weren't my client and if I weren't with Dante...well, he might be the perfect companion for blowing off a little steam.

But he is my client and while I can't say that I'm *with* Dante, I can say that I want to be.

Me, the woman who avoids relationships.

But that's not entirely true, either. I don't really avoid relationships. I've just spent over a decade avoiding them with men other than Dante.

"Brenna?"

Michael is looking at me, his arm outstretched to lead me further into his home.

"Sorry. Long, weird day. My mind was wandering."

"Let me take you to dinner. A drink. A bite. Enchanting conversation."

I conjure a provocative smile. "I'd like that. But I think I'd prefer to stay in. Maybe we could just settle for the drink and the conversation. And who knows what else?"

I watch him swallow, and my confidence ratchets up. "Yes," he says. "I think that sounds just fine."

He leads me into a well-lit room that opens onto a terrace. The door is open, letting in a summer breeze. I take a seat on the couch, then put my purse on the coffee table, trying to position it so that the fisheye lens that is camouflaged by the clasp can get the widest view. The purse is only a camera. The audio is coming through the diamond-studded watch that I am wearing today. And there is another camera hidden in the cameo necklace that hangs around my neck.

Michael has gone to the bar and is opening a bottle of wine. "You like Cabernet, I recall?"

"Very much."

I take the glass he offers me, then slip off my shoe and tuck one leg under me so that I am seated almost sideways on the couch. I smile at him as if this is the perfect position, though I know that he would prefer to scoot closer so that his leg could brush my thigh or his arm could go around my shoulder.

"We so rarely get a chance to talk."

"What would you like to talk about?"

"You, of course," I say, but I punctuate the words with a laugh. "Seriously, I've gotten so many pieces for you over the years. Six, isn't it?" I glance around the room. "And I know you're not monogamous." I pause so he can chuckle at the manner in which I've referred to the other people like me he has hired to find various pieces. "I was expecting to walk into a house that felt like a museum. But you have nothing out. Where is it all?"

He grins, just like a little boy. "Would you really like to see?"

"Of course."

He reaches for a television remote on the table, only it turns out not to be for the television. Instead, the push of a button closes the patio doors, then closes the blinds, dropping the room into darkness.

"Michael?"

"Hold on."

A moment later, hidden panels in the wall begin to open to reveal backlit glass cases. I gasp, genuinely surprised, and stand up. "This is incredible," I say as I walk to one of the walls of cases. So many artifacts are hidden within. From ancient coins to statues to jewelry. Some items appear medieval and look as though they were put to good use during the Inquisition. Others appear innocent, but the neatly printed cards beside them have clues as to their nature—*poison, revenge, deceit.*

I glance up at Michael. "There's a theme, isn't there?" I remember what Dante and his partners had said about cursed artifacts.

"I have a passion for acquiring articles with a story. With a curse."

I laugh. "Do you believe in that?"

"Good god, no. But it makes for a fabulous conversation starter."

At that, my laugh is real.

"All right," I say. "Show me the brooch. What's its horrible backstory?"

He leads me to the opposite wall, and there is the brooch, still in the Lucite box that I had put it in for safe travel. I fiddle with my necklace, trying to ensure that the men back on East 63rd Street have a clear view.

"Why is it still packaged?" I ask.

"I'm selling it," he says.

I turn to him with a frown. "You are?" Had the men from Phoenix made another offer? Hadn't he just turned them down cold?

"The buyer's representative is arriving in three days to acquire the piece," he says, confusing me even more.

"Who's the buyer?"

"A group. Also collectors."

I shake my head with a teasing smile, hoping he can't spot my confusion. "Well, I'm surprised you want to part with it. It's so unusual, and you were so dead set on acquiring it." I actually pull off a small pout. "Should my feelings be hurt?"

He steps closer, moving into my personal space. I force myself not to back up.

"This group has access to a number of items I've been trying to acquire for years. Items that are at the heart of some very interesting lore regarding curses and black magic." He eases behind me, his hands on my shoulders. "You see? It's not about money, but about what they can offer me."

He bends so that his breath tickles my neck and ear. "There are more displays in the bedroom," he says gruffly. "Would you like to see?"

I close my eyes as if in satisfaction and desire. "That sounds wonderful," I murmur. "Why don't you lead the way?"

Chapter 7

"Lead the way?" Dante's stomach twisted as her words—her tone—played again in his head, as if on an endless loop. He was jealous. He knew it.

Honestly, he didn't much care.

He leaned in closer and actually smacked the side of the second monitor, as if that would stop her. "She needs to be getting the hell out of there, not playing footsies with loverboy."

"She's playing the role," Raine said, and Dante heard the amusement in his friend's voice. "Ditch too soon and it will look suspicious."

"Fuck that," Dante said. "We need to pull her right now. Three days? That means we need to get in tomorrow morning, extract Merrick, and get the brooch returned by the day after at the latest."

"Agreed."

"We don't have time for her to play games with him." He shot another glance at the bank of monitors. The purse was still aimed at the display case, but the camera around her neck showed that they were approaching a bedroom. He could see the king-sized bed through the open door. And goddamn fucking hell if there weren't lit candles.

The prick had intended to get her back there all the time.

Not that this was any great revelation. But the knowledge that Folsom might touch her—that she might let him, even as part of the scheme—curled unpleasantly in his gut.

No way. They had what they needed. He was shutting this puppy down.

He grabbed his phone and sent a text—*9-1-1*.

Over the speakers, he heard the *ding-dong* of her text message alert. On screen, he saw the perspective shift as she turned back toward the living room.

"Just a second," she said to Folsom. "My assistant's been having some issues with a client. I should make sure there's no crisis."

Smart girl.

She headed back, the purse becoming larger in the first monitor. Then she reached down and withdrew the phone. She was standing in front of the purse cam now, blocking the view of the display cases. But he could see her face, and the relief he saw when she glanced at the message filled him. *She didn't want Folsom. Thank god for that.*

She snatched up the purse, then licked her lips and made a show of furrowing her brow, all the while with her back to Folsom. Dante couldn't stop his grin. Apparently, she was getting into character.

"Michael," she said. "I'm so sorry. It is a crisis." She approached him—hell, she actually pressed a hand against his cheek. "Rain check?"

For a moment, it looked like Folsom was going to argue. Then he just looked sad.

"Sure," he said. "That would be wonderful."

And as Brenna headed for his front door, Dante couldn't help but feel a little bit sorry for the guy.

Not *that* sorry, of course. But a little.

* * * *

The moment I get out of the taxi, the front door to Dante's condo opens, and he steps outside. I hurry toward him, feeling the rush of adrenaline from having accomplished my super-secret spy mission.

"Did you watch?" I ask as I follow him into the brownstone. "It was as easy as pie."

He nods. His expression is tight. Presumably he is still coming off a flood of worry. He'd been concerned that I couldn't pull it off—hell, I'd been a little concerned, too—but the mission had gone seamlessly.

I'm not sure what I had expected. Perhaps that Michael would tell me he didn't share his collections. Or that he would only reveal them for a trade—I strip, he shows me the brooch, which is something that I really wouldn't have liked. Except for the fact that Dante would be watching through the camera. *That* might make it interesting.

I shake my head, feeling a little silly and a lot giddy. "So what now?"

"Raine and Jessica and Pieter are putting together a counterfeit brooch. It won't stand up to scrutiny, but with any luck it will only need to be in that case for a few hours. We'll go in tomorrow morning when he goes for his morning jog. He's religious about that. And then we'll return the brooch in the evening. We've confirmed that he's planning to see a show tomorrow night."

He speaks firmly. Matter-of-factly.

And honestly, I just don't get it. I want someone to share my victory. I'd expected it to be Dante, and I'm not at all sure what his problem is.

I force my thoughts away from him and back to his words, then frown. "You're just going to walk into his apartment? Did you see the security? There's more electronic locks and gadgets than on the space shuttle."

"We've got it under control." Again, his answer is clipped. Curt. Frankly, it's starting to piss me off.

"Fine," I say. "Good for you. But why the hell do you only need it for a few hours?"

"We have our reasons."

"You know what, Dante? Just screw it. I'm going back to my hotel." I turn to head toward the door, but he grabs my arm and pulls me back.

I stand ramrod straight in front of him, practically vibrating with anger.

"It has a microdot," he says. "We need to retrieve it. That's all."

"That is *so* not all." I grind the words out, and they are harsh. They are an accusation.

For a moment, he says nothing. Just meets my eyes. Just breathes.

Then he seems to sag.

Nothing changes. Not his expression, not his posture. But I know this man, and I see the change in him. And when he looks in my eyes, I see the sadness, too. "I didn't like it." His words are flat. Almost cold.

"Like what?"

"You," he says. "With Folsom. I didn't like the way he looked at you. I didn't like the way he touched you. I didn't like the way you flirted with him. And I damn sure didn't like what he intended to do with you in that bed."

"You didn't?" I can't help myself—I'm smiling.

He notices, and the corner of his lip curves up, too. "No. No, I didn't."

He takes a step toward me. "But it doesn't matter what I like, what I didn't like."

I feel my pulse kick up in tempo. "Why not?"

"Because we said we were done." He reaches out, then gently brushes his fingers down my arm. "No more touching." He takes another step toward me, so that there is barely any distance between us at all, and I forget the muscle contractions required to breathe. "No more fucking," he adds.

"That's what we agreed." It takes all of my willpower to form words, and then even more to take a single step toward him. "Those are the rules."

Now there are only inches between us, and I catch the scent of him—soap and aftershave and, oh god yes, the musky scent of arousal.

I glance down and see his cock, hard now inside his jeans. Straining. My cunt is wet and throbbing, and I cannot help myself. I have to relieve some of the pressure.

I drag my teeth over my lower lip, and as I do, I slide my hand down, then cup myself between my legs over the thin material of my skirt.

Inches from me, Dante groans—and that sound of pure, male arousal fuels me. I use my fingers to ease up my skirt. I'm exposing my thigh—a little bit, then a little bit more. And then the edge of my panties. And then all of them.

The pale blue silk is soaked through, so wet that the material clings to my bare pubis, sticking to my vulva, dipping into my folds. I slide my hand slowly up my thigh and then ease my flat palm under the material.

My skin is so hot, my cunt so wet. And right then, all I want to do is fuck myself with him watching. All I want to do is make him crazy—make him come.

I skim my fingers over myself, and the pressure on my clit makes me shiver. I keep going, my fingers gliding over my slick heat, and then I thrust one, two fingers inside. I swallow a moan, my head thrown back, my eyes closed, as I gyrate my hips, pumping my own hand and imagining that it is Dante.

"Oh, baby," he says. "Fuck the rules."

He drops to his knees and one hand goes to my hip, his thumb hooking in the band of my panties. He tugs them down, then uses his other hand to get them all of the way off.

Then he takes my hand, ignoring my groan of both protest and excitement as cool air brushes over me, as arousing as a lover's touch.

Slowly, he sucks on each of my drenched fingers, and the sensation is so intensely erotic that my knees go weak and I have to cling to his shoulder so as not to fall over.

But when he leans forward and laves me with his tongue, I know that I am going to explode. "No," I protest, taking a step back. "Not yet. I want you inside me when I come. Please, Dante. Please, fuck me."

He looks up at me, and I think that he is going to lay me flat right there and thrust his cock hard inside me. And, oh dear god, I hope he does.

Instead he stands, his golden eyes lit like flames. "Upstairs," he says. "I want you in my bed. Naked and spread-eagled, your pale skin against my black sheets. Your hands fisted in the material as I take you. And I want to hear the echo of your scream when you come."

I can't even manage a response. His words have turned my body to liquid lust, and it is all I can do to nod in blissful, eager agreement.

He has an elevator in his brownstone similar to the one next door, and he leads me up to a masculine room with rich leather and dark wood. A huge bed dominates the space, and yes, the bed is made up with black linens.

Beside it a window is open to the courtyard below. Pale yellow light filters up from a lamp below to cast the room in what looks like candlelight.

"Take off your dress," he says. "I want to see you naked."

"Take off your pants," I counter. "I want to see your cock."

He laughs, and the sound washes over me. "Dear god, Brenna, I lo—I love that mouth of yours."

I draw in a ragged breath because we both know what he

intended to say. And it's true for me, too. I still love him. Wildly. Passionately.

I just don't know what that means.

At the moment, I'm not inclined to analyze. I simply want his hands on me, his cock inside me. And as he follows orders and strips, I do the same, grinning at him as we both move fast, as if in silent competition.

He finishes first, and for a moment, I can only stare at him. At the hard perfection of his body.

A little too perfect, actually, because the scar I remember— that I loved tracing—is gone. And I'm not entirely sure how that can be. It is as if he has a fresh coat of skin, and the old, scarred skin was shed and left behind.

That, of course, makes no sense.

Or it makes as much sense as Dante not aging.

He is looking at me warily, as if he knows what I am thinking. I frown, then make a circular motion with my finger. Slowly, he shows me his back. Where there had been five luscious birds inked on his back, now there are six.

"You got another. Why?"

"A reminder," he says.

"Of what?"

"That I shouldn't lose fights."

He turns back around, and now his face is hard, as if he is afraid that I am getting close to some dark secret. Honestly, I think that I am.

I reach out and touch his chest, then run my finger along the long path of the now-missing scar that once ended just above his pubic bone. He shivers in response to my touch, his already hard cock growing harder.

"I don't understand," I say. "How—"

He takes my hand and cups my fingers around his cock. "Is that really what you want to talk about right now?"

Part of me wants to scream *yes, yes,* because something inside me knows that this is so very important. That this is the key.

But the other part of me—the part now holding velvet steel in my hand, the part that is wet and throbbing with desire—can think about nothing but his hands, his lips, his cock.

Slowly, I shake my head. "No. That's not what I want to talk about."

"Then get on the bed."

I slowly draw my hand over his cock, making him moan before stepping back and releasing him. Then I do as he asks. I get on the bed. I spread my arms. And, yes, I spread my legs.

He is looking right at me, and rather than embarrass me, the sight of his eyes trained right at my core only arouses me more, and I give in to my body's urge to move. To wriggle. To let my hips dance and sway in a futile attempt to find satisfaction.

He takes pity on me and moves to the bed. And though I had told him I couldn't wait to have his cock inside me, I cannot deny that the stroke of his hands upon my bare skin coupled with the kisses he now trails up my leg have me writhing with a building, agonizing pleasure.

He laves my clit, then thrusts his tongue inside me with such wild ferocity it makes me buck. He lifts his head and smiles at me, and though I want more, he continues up my body until his mouth closes over my breast and his teeth bite down on my nipple, softly at first, and then hard enough to make me cry out— even as that pain ricochets down my body from breast to cunt.

"Now," he says, and in one swift and confident movement, he has rolled onto his back and is turning me with him. I end up straddling him, my legs on either side of his waist, his cock standing at attention behind me and teasing my ass in a way that is undeniably enticing.

"Fuck me," he says. "As hard as you want. As deep as you want. And keep your eyes open. I want to watch your face as you come."

I whimper a bit, but I don't protest. Instead I rise up, then scoot back so that I am over his cock, the head placed right at my core. I ease down slowly, then harder. Until finally I can't take the tease and I slam my body down hard before rising up on my knees and repeating the process.

It feels incredible. Like fireworks in my womb spreading out to my fingers and toes.

I feel alive and in love, and even in the midst of this wild passion, I know that is a very dangerous way to feel.

At the moment, I don't much care.

I ride him hard, fondling my breasts when he tells me to, playing with my clit when he tells me to do that.

And when he tells me to come, I do that as well, my body primed to his demands and desires. So yes, I explode on top of him, my body drawing him in, milking him, taking him all the way to his own, violent, explosion.

After, I collapse forward on him and breathe deep, recovering from the power of what just crashed through me. It was more than sex, more than an orgasm. It was a communion, and I am not sure that I can ever be the same.

His arms are around me, holding me close, and we lay like that for a long, long time.

But once the tremors of the orgasm have faded, I slide out of his embrace and pad naked to the window. I hug myself and look down at the courtyard we'd passed through yesterday to get to his office. He's told me that there is another courtyard on the other side of Number 36 and another brownstone, and that one is owned by Mal.

I can't help but wonder about the amount of money these men and Phoenix Security command, or about what they do. In truth, I know very little about them. But I know my heart. And I know what—and who—I want.

I also know what I fear, because I will not survive being tossed away again.

"Brenna?"

I turn to see Dante propped up in bed.

"Are you okay?"

I shake my head. "I should probably go."

He stands up and comes to me. "Talk to me."

I raise a brow. "Talk to you? What is there to talk about? You almost said you loved me—no, don't try to deny it. But, dammit Dante, you've also told me you're going to walk away. You told me that day at the Algonquin, and nothing has changed. And I don't want to lose you again. *Dammit.*"

I didn't mean to spill all of that, much less these damned tears. But it's the truth, and I have no interest in skirting around my feelings. Not now. Not when I have him back in my life.

"I know," he says. "But it can't work," he says, and the pain I hear in his voice is so sharp it feels like a knife that is cutting me to ribbons.

"Why?" I demand. "How the hell do you know if we don't try?"

"Try?" He slides out of bed and comes to stand beside me. He clutches tight to my arms. Almost too tight. "Try?" he repeats. "There's no room for risk in this game, Brenna."

I shake my head, not understanding.

"Dammit, don't you get it?" He is still clutching my arms, so tight I anticipate bruises. "I want you, Brenna. I've wanted you from the moment I met you, and I still want you. I want you, and I don't ever want to let you go."

"Don't do this to me again," I say, tears flooding my eyes. "You told me that in London. You said we had an eternal love. A love that spanned time and distance, and all sorts of pretty words. But then you left. You just left."

"Because it can't work," he repeats. His words are so harsh it sounds as though he is spitting them. "It can't fucking work."

"Why not?" I demand. "I love you, Dante. I wish I didn't. The last thirteen years would have been one hell of a lot less lonely if I could have forgotten about you. But I love you, and every moment that I don't have you is like a knife through my heart. You're the one who left—*you*. So dammit, Dante, I want an explanation. You say it won't work? Then you need to tell me why!"

I am screaming, my voice rising with each word. I can't remember ever being so angry. So hurt. "Tell me," I demand. "Tell me right now."

"You want to know? Fine. *This* is the goddamn reason."

As he speaks, he races toward the window and bursts through the glass. And as my scream fills the room, he falls five stories, then lands in a broken heap in the courtyard below.

Chapter 8

My scream still hangs in the air as I toss my dress over my head and race out of the room and down the stairs.

Oh god oh god oh god...

Another flight, then another.

Oh Christ oh shit...

And again and again until finally I reach the door to the courtyard and I burst through just as Raine and a tall woman with long dark hair race out of the door of Number 36 across from me.

I stare at the woman. I'd seen her only once from a distance, but her image is burned into my mind.

"You?"

She is the woman Dante left me for. And like Dante, she has not aged a day.

"I'm Jessica," she says. "And no. I'm not with Dante. I never was. Trust me, Liam would be pissed."

"Liam?" I think about the huge, gorgeous man with the kind eyes.

"My mate—my husband."

"But—but, Dante said—"

She nods pointedly at his broken body that lies still on the concrete. "He'll explain."

It is those nonsensical words that break the spell. *Shock, I must be in shock.*

"*Explain?*" The word is ripped out of me. "But he's—Oh, god. He needs an ambulance," I cry. "Please, he's—"

"An ambulance won't do him any good. He's dead," Jessica says. "But it will be all right. Trust me. I'm a doctor."

I'm not sure if I should be terrified of this truly crazy woman or feel sorry for her. But I take the chance of turning my back on her and hurry toward Dante. Raine is crouching beside him, but now he stands up and steps away from Dante and toward me, his hand held out as if to stop me.

"You shouldn't go closer," he says.

"The hell I won't." I know he's dead—I can look at him and see that—but I can't make myself believe it. I can't lose him again. Not when I was so close to getting him back. And somehow I know that if I can just hold him then it will turn out that this is all a dream, and—

I try to rush past Raine, but he jerks me to a halt. "Brenna, no. You'll get hurt."

Hurt?

And then, before I have time to ask the question, a wall of flames seems to encircle Dante, the fire moving in to lick at his naked body. Burning away his skin. His beautiful tattoos.

Destroying all that is left of the man I love.

I look at Raine. At Jessica. They are doing nothing about this. If anything, they seem pleased, and all that I can think is that this is crazy. Completely crazy.

I start to scream. To cry. To fall into full-blown, horrible, hysterical grief.

"Brenna, it'll be okay." Jessica's voice is soft beside me, but it is not soothing. I want to hate this woman. This kind woman who presses a hand to my shoulder and says, very gently, "It will be better when you wake. Sleep now, sweetie. Go ahead, just sleep."

I don't want to—I really don't. But my body is so heavy and I start to slip toward the ground.

The last thing I see is Dante's ashes dancing in a circle of fire.

And the last thing I feel is Raine's strong arms going around me and keeping me from collapsing in a heap on the ground.

* * * *

I wake, groggy and disoriented, in Dante's bed, the man himself sitting beside me, studying my face with concern. And with something else that looks like hope.

"Hey," I say as scrub sleep out of my eyes. "I had the most bizarre dream." But even as I say the words, the freakish, impossible truth is settling over me.

It wasn't a dream.

He is wearing pajama bottoms and no shirt. And there is a vibrant phoenix now tattooed on his chest, just over his heart.

I shake my head because none of this makes sense. "Just spit it out," I say. "Please—whatever this is, whatever is going on—it will be easier if you just tell me in one quick burst."

His eyes study mine, and then he nods. "All right," he says. His voice is soft and soothing. "I don't know where to start."

"Anywhere." The word is ripped from me. "I just need words. Please, just start talking because I need your words to ground me."

He seems to understand that because he takes my hand, and I cling tight to it, as if I'm afraid that his words are going to rip him from me.

"I love you," he says, and the words curl around me, warm and comforting. "I should start with that. But it can't—it can't work because I'm immortal. That's what I was trying to tell you. What I had to show you."

I start to say something, but really, there just aren't words. So I close my mouth, and I keep listening.

"I'm not from here—this dimension, this world. None of us are. Me, Raine, Liam, Mal. Jessica. The others—you'll meet them.

We came on a mission from our world, chasing a horrible enemy. We call it the fuerie, and in the chase we were thrown off course. We—and the fuerie—crashed in this dimension."

"When?" It is the only word I can manage.

"About three thousand years ago."

"Oh." I try to process that, but it's too big. So I just nod and latch onto the important part. *Immortal.* Or at least pretty damn close.

"Yes," he agrees when I say as much. "I'm getting there. You see, we are not originally creatures of matter. We're energy. Pure, sentient energy. But we can't exist without form in this dimension. Our essence has to be bound or else it dissipates and we lose our identity. So after we crashed here, we had to find a form."

"So you what? Possessed humans?"

"The fuerie did, yes. They steal bodies. They burn through them. They move through this world spreading evil." He draws a breath. "But that isn't our way. We were met by a group of men and women sent by an Egyptian prince who had visions. He understood what we needed, and we merged with volunteers. Our essence merging with theirs. We became human—and yet not. And, yes, we are immortal. Our bodies do not age. They do not change. And unless we are killed, we go on forever as we are."

"But you just said you're immortal. What do you mean, unless you're killed?"

"You saw it yourself. If we are mortally wounded, we seem to die, but then we are reborn again in the phoenix fire." He points to the seventh tattoo that has appeared on his chest. "With each death, we get a new mark."

I nod slowly. "All right," I finally say.

He looks at me, apparently baffled. "All right?"

"Well, yes." I frown, not sure what he expects.

"You believe me?"

I laugh. "Well, I'd be hard pressed to argue." He's still looking at me as if he is completely gobsmacked. I take his hand. "It's weird, I'll give you that. But it also makes a lot of sense. And—okay, this is going to sound really crazy—but it almost feels like something I knew. But just never realized I knew."

He's still looking at me strangely. Now he shakes his head. "I didn't expect that."

"Why not? Do I seem that close-minded? Like I just toss away evidence that's right in front of my nose?"

"No, no. It's just that such easy acceptance..." He stands and goes to look through the broken window. "We've just always believed it was a sign of—"

I sit up straighter. "Of what?"

He shakes his head. "It doesn't matter." I watch as his shoulders rise and fall, then he turns to face me. "This is why we have to end this. Between us, I mean."

"Oh, I know what you mean. And no."

His brow rises. "No? I don't have a say?"

"Not if I can help it." I slide out of bed and move into his arms. "You're being an ass."

"An ass?" I can't tell if he's amused or annoyed. "I'm trying to protect you. There's no future here. No matter what else might happen, you will grow old, Brenna. You will die. We can't—" His breath hitches. "We can't be together. Not forever."

"Then let's be together for now." My voice is so soft I can barely hear it. "Is that why you pretended with Jessica? To push me away? Because eventually it would end?"

He hesitates, then nods.

"Idiot. Ass. Dumbfuck."

He narrows his eyes at me.

"I mean it. I mean, come on, Dante. I've got at least a few more decades left in me." I frown, struck by the fact that I am in a conversation discussing my own mortality. Not exactly happy fun times.

"You should spend your years with someone you can grow old with."

"Oh, so you'd just toss me aside at the first sign of wrinkles for some tight young thing?" I'm teasing, but the pain in his voice when he answers is real.

"God, no. But—"

I feel the tears burn in my eyes, and I press my palm to his cheek. "Then stop it. Because I want to spend my years with you. So stop worrying about the future. Let's just take the now. We can figure out the rest later." The tears stream freely down my face. "I've missed you so much. You shouldn't have left me. Not because of this."

"It can't last forever," he says. "I thought—" He shakes his head. "God, never mind what I thought. You're here now." He takes my hand and leads me back to the bed.

"Make love to me," I whisper. "We still have a few hours until morning. Make love to me slowly and sweetly. Please," I beg. "Dante, I need you."

His eyes meet mine. "Oh, baby, I need you, too."

Chapter 9

I am still glowing from Dante's touch the next morning as I sip coffee in the VIP lounge of Dark Pleasures.

I've never been here before, but it feels like home. Welcoming, with rich leather and wood and the scent of alcohol and cigars.

Dante brought me with him to his operational meeting with Raine and Mal and Liam.

"I'll run the operation from here," Liam had said. "The three of you will get in and get out fast."

Jessica and Callie and Christina were also there, and Dagny joined us halfway through the meeting.

"Why you three?" I'd asked Dante once the meeting wrapped.

"I'm going because I can detect the fuerie," he said.

"Your enemy? Why would they—"

He cut me off. "We're trying to rescue a brother they trapped. It's reasonable to assume they'll want to stop us. Don't worry," he'd said, seeing my face. "We fight the fuerie all the time—it's what we do. And right now, there aren't any nearby anyway. Besides," he added with a cocky grin, "immortal. Remember?"

I pointed to Mal and Raine. "And those two? They feel the fuerie as well?"

"Mal can manipulate memory. He'll clean up for us afterward

with the security staff, doorman, anyone else we come across. And Raine can talk to electronics. He'll get us into the apartment and then into that display case."

My head was spinning. "Seriously?"

"We're creatures of energy," he said. "That gives us a unique knowledge of how to manipulate that energy. Don't worry," he added before kissing me hard. "The mission will go just fine."

Now, sitting with the women while Liam has gone off to the Phoenix Security office to monitor the action, I can only hope that he was right about the mission going well.

"Relax," Jessica says kindly. "This is what we do, and the coast is clear. No fuerie nearby and Folsom is out for his jog. This mission will be a walk in the park."

I nod, then sit back, holding my coffee tight in both hands because I want the warmth for comfort. I'm trying not to worry—truly—but it's hard.

"So what happens to the man you're trying to rescue?" Maybe if I keep talking, I won't imagine everything that can possibly go wrong.

"If his essence escapes from that gemstone without being bound in another or in a human, then Merrick is essentially dead. So we're going to form an energy field around him. All of the brotherhood gather our energy, then we direct it to pull his essence from the flawed gem and into a pure one."

"So then he just lives in a new gem forever?"

Jessica frowns. "Unfortunately, until we find a human willing to merge with him, that's true. He could take over a human's body, but that's not the way we operate. But this way he will still be alive, and I promise you that time doesn't mean the same thing to him as it does to you."

I nod, but I realize I'm hugging myself. All of this is a lot to take in. I let my gaze wander around the room, giving me a little time to think. Across from the chair I'm curled up in, Christina sits cross-legged on a sofa, her eyes closed, her wrists resting on her knees.

I lean toward Jessica, who I've come to consider my personal instructor. "What's she doing?"

"She can see the fuerie. But it's different than Dante. She has to call up a map in her mind. Great for intelligence. Less practical in the midst of a mission."

I watch, and Jessica is right. It looks like Christina is watching a movie in her mind.

After a moment, she opens her eyes. "All clear," she says and sets a timer on her phone for thirty minutes. "No fuerie on Manhattan, and none for miles."

"So how does it work for Dante?" I ask.

"He can just reach out with his mind. He doesn't have to call up a map. So it's much faster. But he can only feel the fuerie if they are nearby. Christina sees a map of the entire world."

"Wow."

"Pretty much," Jessica agrees.

"He'll look, right?" I ask. "During the mission, I mean. He'll keep reaching out?" I can't shake the feeling that something bad is going to happen.

"Of course." Jessica's voice is soft. Tender. "That's his job. He'll be fine." She takes my hand. "I'm glad you two are back together. In London, he was so gone over for you. I don't think I'd ever seen him so happy, and I've known Dante for a very long time."

"Then why did he leave? Why did you two pretend to be a couple?"

"It's hard," Jessica says. "Everybody wants a forever kind of love, us most of all, because to us, forever is so very real. And when he got through his head that he couldn't have that with you, he tossed away happiness in the now because he couldn't have it in the forever."

"But I love him," I say. "And he loves me. Why wouldn't he just be grateful for the time we could have?"

She lifts a shoulder. "I think he was a little hurt. He'd thought you were truly his—that you really could be his forever. But that's so rare that he shouldn't have even let the possibility enter his mind."

"It's hard not to," Dagny puts in, even as I'm trying to figure out what exactly we're talking about. "I mean, I felt that punch when I met Braydon, and for a while I fantasized that he might really be my mate. But it was just that sexual attraction. Awesome and wonderful and I love him to death, but he's not my forever guy."

"I wish he was," Christina says. "He's my best friend, and I hate the thought that I'm going to live forever and I won't have him to talk to even in just a hundred short years."

My head is spinning. "Wait. Wait, you guys are saying that sometimes mortals really can stay with you forever?"

The three glance at each other, then at me. It's Jessica who speaks. "I thought Dante explained everything to you last night."

"He explained a lot," I say. "This, not so much."

"Shit."

"Tell me," I demand. "What are you talking about?"

Jessica meets Dagny's eyes, and the other girl nods. For a moment, I think that Jessica is going to ignore this tacit permission, but then Jessica draws in a breath. "In our world, finding your mate is a permanent thing. It's more than a bond. It's like a merging. So it's very rare for someone from our dimension to truly mate with a human. But sometimes—very rarely—a true mate is found. It's like what you call soul mates, only more so."

"Okay," I say, certain that Dante is absolutely my soul mate. "But how does a human soul mate live forever?"

"If a human goes into the phoenix fire," Dagny says, "she'll die. Burn up. End of story. But if that human enters her true mate's phoenix fire, she'll be transformed. She'll become immortal. She'll be bound with him and will become one of us."

I'm trying to process all of that. "Wait. Are you saying that if

I'd gone into that fire last night, I could be immortal now? That I could be with Dante forever? Why the hell did you stop me?"

"Because you're not his true mate," Jessica says flatly, her words sitting like rocks in my stomach. "You're not truly his."

"The hell I'm not." A slow burn of fury is rising in me. Not only did they not tell me about the fire that could have brought Dante and I together forever, now they're telling me that we're not really meant to be. "Are you saying he doesn't love me enough?"

Surely not. I've seen the passion in his eyes. Felt it in his touch. But if that's true—oh, god, please let it not be true—then I need to know. Because what I feel with him is so over the top and out of control that I cannot even imagine a world in which he doesn't love me just as deeply.

"He's head over heels for you," Jessica says. "But there's no shame in your not feeling the same way. You can be feel all that and still not be someone's true mate. I mean, seven times before a woman has believed she loved one of the brothers that completely, but she ended up perishing in the flame, anyway."

Christina's timer starts to beep, as if underscoring these awful words.

Dagny shivers. "It was horrible. Only one has ever been a true mate and became immortal. There may have been others, but none willing to risk the fire." She shrugs. "But if they don't want the risk, maybe it's not true."

I'm not interested in these horror stories. They don't apply to me; I'm certain of it. "What makes you think I don't love him enough? That we're not connected enough?"

Dagny and Jessica exchange looks. "He saw you, Brenna. He saw you kissing another man."

It takes me a second, and then I realize what she is talking about. I shake my head, horrified. "What, Rob? He's nothing. No one. He had a crush on me, and I was so scared about the magnitude of what I was feeling for Dante that I let him kiss me.

But it meant nothing. I felt nothing."

I drag my fingers through my hair. "Why didn't he say something back then? Hell, why didn't he ask me about it now?"

Jessica sighs. "Oh, sweetie, do you think he could stand knowing he'd lose you? You had doubts. Even if you swear that you didn't—and even if you mean it—your uncertainty must have been there, buried deep. Better to end it fast and hard and walk away than to suffer and then lose each other."

I shake my head vehemently. "No. No doubts. I love Dante," I say. "I always have."

"I believe you believe that. But love doesn't necessarily mean—and what we're talking about—the depth of emotion—it's so big. And if you were scared, having doubts..."

She trails off, looking as miserable as I feel.

"I would survive the fire," I say. "I'm sure of it."

Dagny and Jessica exchange another glance. "I'm sorry," Jessica finally says. "But I'm not sure at all."

A few feet from us, Christina's eyes fly open and she jerks, as if thrown out of a trance. *"The fuerie,"* she says. "I have no idea how they got to the city so quickly. But they're here—and it looks like they're heading to Folsom's house."

Chapter 10

"*Fuerie*," Dante cried. "They're converging. Finish it up and lets get the hell out of here."

"Got it." Raine said, sliding the gemstone into the bag he wore around his waist. "We're good to go."

"How long?" Mal asked.

"They're moving fast," Dante said. "A car. Motorcycles. Not sure. But there's no reason to think they know about us. They're coming to do the same thing—steal the gem with Merrick from Folsom."

"His buyer who could supply cursed artifacts," Raine said with a snort. "Fuck that. Poor guy doesn't even know the scum he's dealing with."

They hurried out, with Mal doing whatever memory manipulation he had to in order to clean up the trail they were blazing.

The Phoenix Security SUV was right outside the building, and Dennis, their driver, had the engine revving. Raine climbed in first, then Mal.

Dante was about to do the same when Jessica's Ferrari skidded to a stop across Fifth Avenue, to the consternation of nearby cars and taxis.

"Brenna!" She called to Dante from across the street.

"Christina told us about the fuerie, and she took off running. This way. To find you."

Fuck.

"Go," he shouted to Dennis, then slammed the door to the SUV. Not one to question authority, Dennis peeled away from the curb and disappeared back toward Number 36.

"I'll help you find her," Jessica said as she abandoned the car and raced across the street toward him.

"No. Merrick's too far gone. Get to Number 36. Do the ritual without me. Do it now, Jessica, before we lose him. Get Merrick safe. I'll take care of Brenna."

She hesitated, then nodded. "Be careful," she said. "There are fuerie around."

"I know the danger." And he did. Even though the brothers' bodies couldn't die, after enough deaths, their souls were burned out of them, rendering them hollow. Empty. Mad.

The fuerie knew that, too. And took great pleasure in seeking the death of the brothers.

But that wasn't even Dante's first concern. Because the fuerie were like feral beasts, and they would smell the scent of a brother on her. And if they did, they would kill her simply because she belonged to him.

Brenna.

Oh, god, Brenna.

* * * *

I do not know why I am running, I only know that I have to. That it seems foolish, but it is not.

Because I know by some sixth sense I trust that this is my chance to have him. To save him. To save us.

And so I race down Fifth Avenue, silently thanking my Pilates instructor because at least I'm not completely winded, though I do have one hell of a stitch in my side.

But I can't stop. I have to find him. Have to hold him. Have to look him in the eye and tell him that he is a huge asshole. A prick. A complete and total dumbfuck.

Because how the hell could he not know the depth of my feelings?

Then again, I didn't understand my feelings either, which was why I let Rob kiss me.

So clearly I'm just as much of a dumbfuck.

Apparently, we really are meant for each other. A perfect pair.

The thought makes me giddy and I run faster—then quicken my pace even more when I hear my name and see him in the distance.

He's running toward me from the opposite direction, and for one brief, surreal moment it feels like we are living in a movie. A sappy romance, and soon he will grab me around the waist and swing me around and the soundtrack will swell.

Except, of course, this is not a movie. Or if it is, it's not a romance. Because just as he is about to cross the street to reach my block, someone tall and muscular tackles me from the side, and we go down hard.

"Bitch!"

I kick, getting the bastard in the face, and then race down the street toward Dante, screaming his name.

He runs to me and grabs my hand. "Fuerie," he says, then makes a sharp right turn into an alley between two residential buildings.

The man—the fuerie—comes along, too. And apparently they travel in pairs because another one is right there behind him.

I scream because this alley is a dead end and I'm really not sure what else to do.

But then they are attacking, wild and crazy, with swords that seem more like whips but slice through everything. One catches the edge of my ankle and I scream, the pain almost more than I can bear.

He grins, as if the sound makes him happy, and starts to advance toward me.

Beside me, Dante is fighting the other one, who has a whip of his own, but at my cry, he kicks it into high gear. He has a weapon—like a sword of vibrant light. And he is slashing and hacking. I have never seen him fight, and he moves with grace and power, and in no time at all, the fuerie is headless. He stabs the sword through the fuerie's heart, and the dead creature combusts, leaving only a pile of ash.

The other one lets out a wild cry and rushes me. I scream as it raises its whip hand, and Dante leaps in front of me, taking the brunt of the blow, the whip slicing hard across his neck and ripping open his chest.

He falls, his blood staining the asphalt.

I stand in shock. The fuerie is right there, sneering at me. Coming at me.

I grab Dante's sword and I lunge, terror taking the place of skill. And though I do not know how I do it, somehow I manage to take the fuerie down. And then, with a burst of satisfaction, I drive Dante's sword through the creature's heart.

"Baby." Dante's voice is weak, and I kneel beside him.

"You fool," I say, as tears stream down my face. "How could you not believe? How could you not know? Of course I love you. Of course I'm yours. I always have been. And I always will be."

He shakes his head. "No, too risky. Doubt. That man. Don't do it." His eyes meet mine. "Don't do it."

But I know that I will. I know that I have to.

More than that, I cannot wait.

I take his sword, and I look my love in the eyes. And then I stand over his fallen body, one leg on either side of his waist. "I love you," I say as I thrust the sword down and through his heart. "And now I'm going to prove it."

* * * *

Pain.

And the sickening smell of burning flesh.

I am standing in a firestorm. The world and my body alight.

And with every tiny ounce of sanity within me I want to leap out of this circle. I want to run to the hospital and let them treat my burns.

I am immolating myself, and the pain—oh, the pain rips through me like talons, tearing my insides out, melting me, destroying me.

I try to gasp. To breathe, but the fire burns my throat. I am dying, I am living.

I am life and death all twisted around into one thing. One horrible, painful, writhing thing.

And then I am going. Death taking. The world darkening.

Fear wells in me, and I try to reach out. Try to call his name.

Because I am afraid that I am leaving now. That it is over.

That I have made a mistake.

And that I will never see Dante again.

Chapter 11

I'm alive.

I'm breathing, and I'm alive, and I'm his.

Joy sweeps through me, and I open my eyes to see Dante smiling over me. "You stupid woman," he says, and I hear the fear in his voice. "You stupid, stupid woman." He pulls me to him, hugging me tight even as I hug him right back. "You could have burned to death."

"No," I say. I pull back so that I can see his eyes, then I slowly tug down the neck of the nightgown that someone has dressed me in to reveal the new small phoenix now inked on my shoulder. "See? I couldn't have."

His laugh sounds a lot like a muffled cry.

And then he kisses me, hard and hungry, and it feels as though he has never kissed me before. And honestly, I suppose he really hasn't. We're bound now, truly together, in a way that we have never been before.

I'm his, and he is mine. *Forever.*

It sounds so long.

Hell, it sounds so wonderful.

I break the kiss, then press my palms flat against his shirt before looking up to meet his eyes. "Touch me," I say. "Take me."

His slow smile is all the answer I need, and I shift as he pulls the sheet back, then lift my hips so that he can peel the nightgown off me. I'm wearing nothing underneath, my clothes having burned away in the phoenix flame.

He bends to me, then presses his lips to the phoenix that now marks my shoulder. The sensation of his lips on my skin seems to cut through me, sweet and wondrous. As if it is a map of circuits and he has suddenly lit me up.

But he is not satisfied with that.

Slowly, and so deliciously sweetly, he starts to trail kisses all over my body, his ministrations setting me on fire. Again, I think, and then I laugh.

He looks up. "What?"

"You're setting me on fire," I say, and his laugh joins with mine.

"I'll do more than that."

He turns back to his task with focused determination. His hands hold my legs apart, and he very thoroughly kisses his way up my legs, then slowly—so painfully slowly—teases my sex with his tongue.

"Please," I beg. "Please, I need you inside me. I need to feel you."

"I know, baby. Me, too." He straddles me, then slowly enters me, stretching and filling me until I can't tell where he ends and I begin. We rock together, and it's not frantic or wild, but gentle and sweet and wonderful. So many ways to touch him, to know him. And we have barely even scratched the surface.

"I can't hold back," he says. "I have to feel you."

"Never hold back," I say. "Not with me."

His response is a low groan, and he thrusts hard into me, then faster and faster until the pressure builds between us and we explode together, our bodies and our souls twined as one.

I make a soft noise of satisfaction and go completely limp. "Mmm." That is about the only sound I can manage.

He chuckles and pulls me close, and we stay like that for a moment, simply feeling. Simply enjoying.

"They were able to save Merrick?" I ask after a few moments, my eyes heavy.

"They were."

"Who will he merge with?"

"I don't know," Dante says. "Someone extraordinary. But he's safe now. He's safe because of you."

I roll over so that I am straddling him, then use my finger to trace the outline of another newly inked phoenix on his breast. "We wasted so much time. Thirteen years lost because I was a fool, too scared to believe that I'd really found true love."

"Don't look at it that way," he says. "Think of what could have happened if you'd walked away from me that first night in London. Or if you'd refused to help me when I found you in the Algonquin. So many things tried to drive us apart, Brenna. But it was love that pulled us back together. Don't mourn those thirteen years," he says, brushing his thumb gently under my eye to wipe away an errant tear.

"They're just a blip," he says. "And baby, we have all the time in the world waiting for us."

A note from JK

I hope you enjoyed *Caress of Pleasure!*

Be sure not to miss any of the stories in the Dark Pleasures series:

Caress of Darkness (Callie and Raine's story)
Find Me in Darkness (Mal and Christina, part 1)
Find Me in Pleasure (Mal and Christina, part 2)
Find Me in Passion (Mal and Christina, part 3)
Caress of Pleasure (Dante and Brenna's story)

Learn more at my website, http://www.juliekenner.com

And be sure to subscribe to my newsletter so you don't miss a thing: http://bit.ly/JK_newsletter

Sign up for the 1001 Dark Nights Newsletter
and be entered to win a Tiffany Key necklace.

There's a new contest every month!

Go to www.1001DarkNights.com to subscribe.

As a bonus, all subscribers will receive a free
1001 Dark Nights story
The First Night
by Lexi Blake & M.J. Rose

Turn the page for a full list of the
1001 Dark Nights fabulous novellas...

1001 Dark Nights

WICKED WOLF by Carrie Ann Ryan
A Redwood Pack Novella

WHEN IRISH EYES ARE HAUNTING by Heather Graham
A Krewe of Hunters Novella

EASY WITH YOU by Kristen Proby
A With Me In Seattle Novella

MASTER OF FREEDOM by Cherise Sinclair
A Mountain Masters Novella

CARESS OF PLEASURE by Julie Kenner
A Dark Pleasures Novella

ADORED by Lexi Blake
A Masters and Mercenaries Novella

HADES by Larissa Ione
A Demonica Novella

RAVAGED by Elisabeth Naughton
An Eternal Guardians Novella

DREAM OF YOU by Jennifer L. Armentrout
A Wait For You Novella

STRIPPED DOWN by Lorelei James
A Blacktop Cowboys ® Novella

RAGE/KILLIAN by Alexandra Ivy/Laura Wright
Bayou Heat Novellas

DRAGON KING by Donna Grant
A Dark Kings Novella

PURE WICKED by Shayla Black
A Wicked Lovers Novella

HARD AS STEEL by Laura Kaye
A Hard Ink/Raven Riders Crossover

STROKE OF MIDNIGHT by Lara Adrian
A Midnight Breed Novella

ALL HALLOWS EVE by Heather Graham
A Krewe of Hunters Novella

KISS THE FLAME by Christopher Rice
A Desire Exchange Novella

DARING HER LOVE by Melissa Foster
A Bradens Novella

TEASED by Rebecca Zanetti
A Dark Protectors Novella

THE PROMISE OF SURRENDER by Liliana Hart
A MacKenzie Family Novella

FOREVER WICKED by Shayla Black
A Wicked Lovers Novella

CRIMSON TWILIGHT by Heather Graham
A Krewe of Hunters Novella

CAPTURED IN SURRENDER by Liliana Hart
A MacKenzie Family Novella

SILENT BITE: A SCANGUARDS WEDDING by Tina Folsom
A Scanguards Vampire Novella

DUNGEON GAMES by Lexi Blake
A Masters and Mercenaries Novella

AZAGOTH by Larissa Ione
A Demonica Novella

NEED YOU NOW by Lisa Renee Jones
A Shattered Promises Series Prelude

SHOW ME, BABY by Cherise Sinclair
A Masters of the Shadowlands Novella

ROPED IN by Lorelei James
A Blacktop Cowboys ® Novella

TEMPTED BY MIDNIGHT by Lara Adrian
A Midnight Breed Novella

THE FLAME by Christopher Rice
A Desire Exchange Novella

CARESS OF DARKNESS by Julie Kenner
A Dark Pleasures Novella

Also from Evil Eye Concepts:

TAME ME by J. Kenner
A Stark International Novella

THE SURRENDER GATE by Christopher Rice
A Desire Exchange Novel

Bundles:

BUNDLE ONE
Includes Forever Wicked by Shayla Black
Crimson Twilight by Heather Graham
Captured in Surrender by Liliana Hart
Silent Bite by Tina Folsom

BUNDLE TWO
Includes Dungeon Games by Lexi Blake
Azagoth by Larissa Ione
Need You Now by Lisa Renee Jones
Show My, Baby by Cherise Sinclair

About Julie Kenner

J. Kenner (aka Julie Kenner) is the *New York Times, USA Today, Publishers Weekly, Wall Street Journal* and #1 International bestselling author of over seventy novels, novellas and short stories in a variety of genres.

Though known primarily for her award-winning and international bestselling erotic romances (including the Stark and Most Wanted series) that have reached as high as #2 on the *New York Times* bestseller list, JK has been writing full time for over a decade in a variety of genres including paranormal and contemporary romance, "chicklit" suspense, urban fantasy, and paranormal mommy lit.

Her foray into the latter, *Carpe Demon: Adventures of a Demon-Hunting Soccer Mom* by Julie Kenner, has been consistently in development in Hollywood since prior to publication. Most recently, it has been optioned by Warner Brothers Television for development as series on the CW Network with Alloy Entertainment producing.

JK has been praised by *Publishers Weekly* as an author with a "flair for dialogue and eccentric characterizations" and by *RT Bookclub* for having "cornered the market on sinfully attractive, dominant antiheroes and the women who swoon for them." A four time finalist for Romance Writers of America's prestigious RITA award, JK took home the first RITA trophy awarded in the category of erotic romance in 2014 for her novel, *Claim Me* (book 2 of her Stark Trilogy).

Her books have sold well over a million copies and are published in over over twenty countries.

In her previous career as an attorney, JK worked as a clerk on the Fifth Circuit Court of Appeals, and practiced primarily civil, entertainment and First Amendment litigation in Los Angeles and Irvine, California, as well as in Austin, Texas. She currently lives in Central Texas, with her husband, two daughters, and two rather spastic cats.

Say My Name

Don't miss Say My Name, the first book in the new Stark International trilogy by J. Kenner!

I never let anyone get too close—but he's the only man who's ever made me feel alive.

Meeting Jackson Steele was a shock to my senses. Confident and commanding, he could take charge of any room . . . or any woman. And Jackson wanted me. The mere sight of him took my breath away, and his touch made me break all my rules.

Our bond was immediate, our passion untamed. I wanted to surrender completely to his kiss, but I couldn't risk his knowing the truth about my past. Yet Jackson carried secrets too, and in our desire we found our escape, pushing our boundaries as far as they could go.

Learning to trust is never easy. In my mind, I knew I should run. But in my heart, I never felt a fire this strong—and it could either save me or scorch me forever.

* * * *

"I want to know why you ended it."

My chest tightens and I have to resist the urge to hug myself. I can feel the anxiety reaching for me even now, along with the nightmares and twisted memories that slink along, too. Slithering out of the night to fill my days. I shake my head, determined to keep it all banished, far and away. "It doesn't matter."

He turns from the window, his face a wild mixture of anger and hurt. "The hell it doesn't."

"My reasons are my own, Jackson." I can hear the panic creeping into my voice, and I fear that he can as well. Deliberately, I take slow, even breaths. I want to calm myself. And, damn me, I want to soothe him.

I want to ease the hurt that I caused, but that's impossible, because I can't answer his question.

"Why?" he asks again, only now there's a gentleness in his voice that unnerves me.

I stiffen in automatic defense, afraid I'll melt in the face of any tenderness from this man. "You didn't want to end it," Jackson continues. "Even now, you want it."

"You have no idea what I want," I say sharply, though that is a lie as well.

"Don't I?" There is anger in his voice. Hurt, too. "I know you want the resort."

I've been looking at the tabletop, and now I lift my head. "Yes." The word is simple. It may be the first completely true thing I've said to him since Atlanta. "Will you take it? You and I both know it's the opportunity of a lifetime. Are you really going to let our past stand in the way of what can be a truly magnificent achievement?"

I watch his shoulders rise and fall as he takes a breath. Then he turns away from me to look out the window once again. "I want the project, Sylvia."

Relief sweeps over me, and I have to physically press my hands to the table to forestall the urge to leap to my feet and embrace him.

"But I want you, too." He turns as he speaks, and when he faces me straight on, there is no denying the truth—or the longing—in his eyes.

I swallow as what feels like a swarm of electric butterflies dances over my skin, making the tiny hairs stand up. And making me aware of everything from the solidity of the floor beneath my feet to the breath of air from a vent across the room.

I force myself to remain seated. Because damn me, my instinct is to go to him and slide into his arms. "I—I don't understand." The lie lingers in the air, and I am proud of the way I kept my voice from shaking.

"Then let me be perfectly clear." He closes the distance between us, then uses his forefinger to tilt my head up so that he is looking deep into my eyes. I shift, not only because the contact sends a jolt of electricity right through me, but because I'm afraid that if he looks too deeply into my eyes, he will see a truth I want to keep hidden.

"No," he says. "Look at me, Sylvia. Because I'm not going to say this again. I told you once that I'm a man who goes after what he wants, and I want you in my bed. I want to feel you naked and hot beneath me. I want to hear you cry out when you come, and I want to know that I am the man who took you there."

On behalf of 1001 Dark Nights,

Liz Berry and M.J. Rose would like to thank ~

Steve Berry
Doug Scofield
Kim Guidroz
Jillian Stein
Dan Slater
Asha Hossain
Chris Graham
Pamela Jamison
Jessica Johns
Richard Blake
BookTrib After Dark
and Simon Lipskar

CPSIA information can be obtained
at www.ICGtesting.com
Printed in the USA
LVOW03s2213120218
566263LV00001B/35/P